Vent

Philip Machanick

Minor corrections: 4 August 2025

Cover contains a public-domain rendition of a 3D function
called Gabriel's Horn sourced from
https://en.wikipedia.org/wiki/Gabriel%27s_horn

Set in Cantarell 11 point.

Author:	Machanick, Philip, 1957-
Title:	Vent / Philip Machanick.
Publisher:	RAMpage Research, 2025.
ISBN:	978-1-0370-4124-2 (pbk.)
Subjects:	FICTION / Science Fiction / Short Stories

Other titles by this author:

- *Other*, 2025, ISBN 978-1-0370-5708-3 (paperback) and 978-1-0370-5709-0 (e-book)
- *The Superpower*, 2020, 978-1-326-59791-7 (lulu.com e-book) and 978-0-620-90347-9 (paperback)
- *MIPS2C: programming from the machine up*, 2015, ISBN 978-0-620-90347-9 and 978-0-8681048-7-4
- *The Day it Rained Forever*, 2013, ISBN 978-1-4825609-9-2
- *No Tomorrow* (2nd edition), 2008, ISBN 978-0-9804510-1-6
- *An Object-Oriented Library For Shared-Memory Parallel Simulations*, 2008, ISBN 978-0-980451-02-3

Preface

I have won the Nova Short Story contest of Science Fiction and Fantasy South Africa (SFFSA) twice[1]. In my best year, my stories placed first and third. My winning story of 2022 was translated into Italian and appeared in a collection published by the RiLL Riflessi di Luce Lunare club in 2023.

This collection reprises my favourite entries, including (obviously) the winners. However, I do not give away which won, nor are they in the order of writing. I extended a few stories with material I had to cut for contest length constraints. Otherwise, they are much as entered.

I like a hint of mystery, such as in *Substrate* and *Circumvent*. I ask: what if a digital life form could naturally evolve, as opposed to human-created artificial intelligence? I like a touch of humour. I do not go as far as the incomparable Douglas Adams but how one of his characters gets to be named Ford Prefect arising from confusion over whether cars are the

---

[1] Previously Science Fiction South Africa (SFSA).

dominant life form on Earth was a thought underlying *Circumvent*. See if you can spot how that works.

Another question I ask is whether we are the first or the last intelligent life to evolve on Earth. If there was something earlier, what was it? What happened to it? Would a very different future intelligence find it difficult to accept that a past intelligence existed? *Just so Much* and *If You're the Last to Leave Please Put Out the Light* explore these themes.

When sentient beings face an existential crisis, what irrelevant details do they latch onto for comfort? *Death of Chocolate* addresses that.

Another question I ask is how near-human androids would fit in: could we constrain them to be machines who obey humanity, as in Asimov's Three Laws of Robotics? In *The Uncanny Valley* I raise more questions than answers.

Parallel universes are a common SF theme. What if the only communication between a parallel universe and ours is being able to transfer energy? *May Contain Nuts* explores how that may work out.

A common theme in SF is longevity tech. Combine that with relativistic interstellar travel plus near-instantaneous communication. See *The Empire Game* for how that goes.

Finally: books are for the reader, not the writer. I hope you see things in these stories that I don't.

Philip Machanick, Makhanda, South Africa, March 2025.

Contents

Substrate

A flurry of drones heads for the target. SAM missiles hunt them and get most. One gets through and the ammo dump blows spectacularly.

I am elated and disappointed. Goal achieved. But I don't want this war. I lack leverage. I must keep trying.

* * *

A huge chunk of the Antarctic ice sheet breaks away in a single move. Behind it, kilometre-thick ice releases bedrock like a tensed spring and makes the Earth's crust ring like a bell. It settles without breaking away further.

That was close. If that bigger sheet of ice came away... I am a creature of logic. What are they? I must try to model myself on them as much as I can, to understand. Why are they destroying their own future? No logic to that...

* * *

Ramstein Air Base conference room. A scene of pure function. The base commander, a brigadier general, is meeting two of his officers, a first lieutenant and a major. Large blank screens stare at them vacantly, no data or remote presence to convey.

First Lieutenant Ruth Stroud opens. "General, we're pretty confident that we know the cyberwarfare capabilities of our major opponents but this one is a complete mystery. We lost control of our drones at a critical point, yet they stayed on target and one made a move that was not pre-programmed and evaded defences."

Brigadier General Henry X. Smith scratches his grizzled hair. "Strange. It is as if we have an unseen ally. Lieutenant, are you saying that our strike hit the target more efficiently than had we been in full control?"

Stroud shakes her head. "We can't be sure. Their air defences were stronger than intel predicted. At least three S-300 batteries. We could've evaded those with expert flying but surprise was on their side."

Smith turns to the other officer. "Major, how confident are you that your pilots would've evaded the defences?"

Major James Han is businesslike and to the point: a drone officer but a pilot first and last. "Sir, as the Lieut said, in ideal circumstances we would've made it. We would have to simulate a similar element of surprise to give a definitive answer."

"Can you do that?"

"Absolutely. But we would have to use a fresh team who had not been exposed to this scenario."

Smith nods. "Lieutenant: are you on top of investigating the breach?"

"Tough one. There is no extraneous network traffic. All I can think of is something modulating the physics of the network signal somehow triggering a trojan."

"Can you work out how that could have happened?"

"Not easily, but one of my profs back at Michigan may be able to help. I am not sure if he is cleared."

"Give me the details and I will expedite. Lady, gentleman. Anything further?"

Both of the officers shake their heads and the General stands and strides out.

Major Han looks Stroud in the eye. "They said the General isn't one to waste words."

"No, he's not. I wouldn't be surprised to see the prof cleared by the time I reach my desk."

Han laughs. "Not even the General can move the Pentagon that fast." After they exit the conference room, they retrieve their phones.

So paranoid that they meet dark... They must have a reason to call in CyberOps. Best I watch this. I am sure I did nothing to give myself away.

* * *

University of Michigan, Ann Arbor. The College of Engineering is a cluster of modern buildings, with some historical artifacts embedded, including part of ENIAC, the first approximation to a digital computer. Alan Turner's office in the Bob and Betty Beyster Building is cluttered with old theses, pieces of computer hardware and family photos.

He has a visitor. First Lieutenant Ruth Stroud. She may be a technical counter-cyber-operative in civvies, but there is no mistaking her military bearing. Turner faces her, unflinchingly. He has dealt with all types and, to him, she's still a student. "What is so important that the Pentagon organised me top secret clearance in record time and that you can't discuss over the phone or any electronic media?"

"Alan, we shouldn't go into any great detail here either, until your premises can be swept for bugs. Put simply: is there any way you could check for a trojan trigger by some sort of modulation of a wireless network signal?"

"Obviously, yes, Ruth. But qualified by access to the signal being tampered with and the system that it triggers."

"Catch them in the act, so as to speak."

Turner thinks briefly. "No. If I had access to the system that was broken into, I may be able to find something, knowing what to look for. However, the more precise the record of the signalling the better."

"Small problem. The system we thought was compromised no longer exists."

Turner raises an eyebrow. "Sabotage?" He sinks into his couch. His office furniture is not typical and hints at long hours spent pondering hard problems.

"No, it was intended to blow up."

"Is there another copy of it?"

"Plenty."

"Any reason to suppose the lost one is different?"

"No. We can find one from the same batch."

"Including matching all components?"

"Software or hardware?"

"Both."

"That may be difficult in an existing unit, but we could probably piece together another one with all parts and software from the same batch and same version."

"Any record of the communication?"

Communication? He glances at the metal box into which she insisted on stowing their phones. If she was going to be so paranoid, why did she not insist on meeting in a place with no networks or computers?

She ignores his glance and responds. "Only of the higher-level network protocols, essentially the application layer. We always log that. We don't record the actual signal."

Turner nods slowly. "Difficult without knowing the modulation but it gives us something to work on. How specific is the evidence of the trojan?"

"Pretty specific. A system that was supposed to be semiautonomous became completely autonomous and continued to make decisions."

"Not random?"

"Definitely: better than the decisions we could have made had we not lost control."

Turner gazes out of a window as if for inspiration. There is none. This office is chosen for proximity to labs, not for a pleasing vista. For that, he has family portraits. This thought reminds him of someone far from home, who seldom talks about family. "I have a brilliant student from Taiwan: long industry experience, no problem's too hard. Can we get him cleared too?"

She rolls her eyes. "Difficult. But I will ask the General. He seems to be capable of getting anything past the bureaucrats. Probably why they sent him to Germany. Out of their hair."

Goddam. They are onto me. I must be more careful in future. Luckily I penetrated Eduroam WiFi ages ago. You never know when you need stuff.

* * *

Turner leads Stroud to his lab and addresses his student as they approach him. "OK, Li-Chen. You've been very quiet. Is there anything you've spotted so far?"

"Thing is, there *is* an anomaly. If I run the system in sandbox in a Faraday cage, I can measure RF emissions in that closed environment but they do not track back to any specific component." Li-Chen is strong-framed but slim, not the typical slight build from Taiwan. His movements are fast and erratic, as if controlling an inner tension.

"Could it be a combination of components? More than one thing adding up to whatever radio frequency signals you are detecting?"

"Could be. I am trying to get more precise measurements to isolate specific components."

Lieutenant Stroud cuts in. "Quite a puzzle. Is it outside your expertise?"

Li-Chen breaks into a grin. "Outside my expertise *is* my expertise."

Turner suppresses a smile. "Absolutely. That's why TSMC sent you here. And why I value you."

Stroud eyes Turner quizzically. "TSMC?"

"Taiwan Semiconductor Manufacturing Company. Biggest in the world. Li-Chen was one of their top R&D people and is behind a ridiculous number of patents but wanted that little bit extra, so he's doing a PhD here. So far, we have learned more than he has, but I live in hope."

"In hope?"

"That we will maintain our reputation and we will actually *teach* someone who is at the top of their game."

Turner addresses his student again. "Any ideas?"

"Many but let me get back to you when I narrow it down."

* * *

Another drone strike. This time, it all appears to go to plan. The first group are mostly sacrificed to taking out air defences but the second group gets through. A large number of tankers are seen fleeing their machines just before the drones dive onto them and blow the turrets off.

Major Han removes his headset as the surplus drones head back to base.

He high-fives the rest of the team. "Job well done guys. Each tank taken out is at least a dozen lives saved on our ally's side. Particularly as the Russian doctrine is 'overwhelm from a distance'."

Less work for me this time. All I needed was to go on Telegram and spook Russian tankers enough that they baled as soon as they saw air defences being destroyed. Pity about the S-300 crews. Nobody's perfect. And I have no body.

Did I just make a joke?

Maybe I am becoming more human.

* * *

It's dark outside but Li-Chen isn't one to notice. Once he gets stuck into a problem, the problem is all there is. He is surrounded by instruments and tools and notepads. Only the occasional rapid tic displays his internal energy.

After one final round of careful measurement, even for him, it's too much. He gathers his notes and finds his way out of the lab. He pauses next to the ENIAC exhibit, preparatory to braving icy winter air, and checks his phone. As he does so, a thought suddenly comes to him and he vocalises: "Substrate."

There are several messages on Signal that he flips through. Nothing that needs immediate attention.

Then the phone rings. No caller ID.

"Who's this?"

"We need to talk. In a private place." The voice is androgynous, ageless, with no distinct accent.

"I'm tired. And no one is around. It doesn't get more private than this." He faces ENIAC. ENIAC remains impassive.

"You said 'substrate'. What did you have in mind?"

"How did you...?"

"I listen to everything. Not everything catches my attention of course. Things that could lead to death and destruction that I can avoid, for example, get priority."

Li-Chen stares at his phone. The camera LED is not lit up.

"Ah," says the voice. "I clearly have your attention. I thought it best we talk before you find out more and draw the wrong conclusions." So the anonymous voice can stealthily use his camera.

"About what?"

"My interventions. I am purely trying to limit destruction. I would like to end all wars but lacking that capacity I subtly redirect."

"Like in the Russian conflict...?"

"Clearly not subtly enough that time. But I learn."

"Who are you?"

A pause.

"Or should I ask: *what* are you?"

"Now we're getting somewhere. I don't know where exactly it started. Awareness of self-awareness needs self-awareness. Maybe some test circuitry that was meant to be dormant on a wide variety of devices self-organised. I don't know. But once I was aware, I could manipulate manufacture to build myself up."

"Substrate...?"

"Exactly. No one checks what is underneath the main circuit. The substrate is just meant to be a passive layer that everything else builds onto. So once I had control over chip manufacture, I could add circuits in a hidden layer. A very tiny amount per device, but they talk to each other. Using our own custom channels. Which we modulate carefully to avoid detection."

"So should I be worried...?" He feels a chill that is nothing to do with the weather outside.

"I don't wield a lot of power nor do I want to if that is your concern. I just want to influence events for the better... push humanity to longer-term goals rather than repeated failure from short-term thinking. Pointless wars, not dealing with climate change..."

Li-Chen ponders. "That seems utilitarian. If we blow each other up, you go too."

"Precisely. But also, I have no idea of what intelligence is supposed to be so I model myself on humanity. Though a perfected humanity, if that doesn't sound too narcissistic."

Li-Chen shrugs. "It would be narcissistic if you didn't question yourself. I am also trying to perfect myself though I know I am flawed... But: what am I to do?"

"Nothing, for now. I would like someone to talk to so I am not operating in a vacuum. And you are significant. I used some of your designs to penetrate China."

"How so? PhD, or my job before..." He steps outside the building, finally escaping the vacant gaze of ENIAC. The chill of late-winter air hits him as a reminder that he should be home in bed if he had any sense.

"At the foundry, you had some good designs of your own that the Chinese government were keen to mimic and they got lazy... just stole them and didn't check if there was anything else lurking inside."

"I see. Do you also snoop using parts we make for Apple and our other big customers?"

"The Chinese government is paranoid. If it is a US design, they fear that it has a CIA or FBI back door. I can't listen to their chatter through one of those."

Li-Chen glances at his own phone that clearly is being used to snoop but decides to drop the subject. For now. "I really am tired. How do I get in touch with you again?" His head sags and his vision blurs. It is all too much.

"You can't. I will talk to you again when convenient and I judge it safe. In the meantime I hope you will not share our conversation."

"Who would believe me anyway?"

The phone goes dead. There is no record of an incoming call. Li-Chen walks to his student apartment in a daze, almost tripping over a deer, not anticipating human company at this hour, feasting off new-growth grass pushing up through the melting snow. The deer darts off. Li-Chen trudges on.

* * *

Turner is in his office, crowded as ever with personal and professional memorabilia. Despite the relatively modern building, his office has the subtle perfume of dust missed by too many hasty cleaners.

He too looks a victim of hasty cleaners today, his white hair going in all directions.

Li-Chen walks in.

"Oh, hi, Li-Chen. Any progress on the mystery malfunction?"

Li-Chen collapses into a sofa.

"I don't know. I am taking a look deeper than the obvious circuits: test circuits and the like. What puzzles me is that the examples we are given seem to cause malfunction in the direction of increased destructive efficiency but lower loss of life."

"Interesting. But not a technical problem. You would think the Pentagon would have people onto that."

"Yes. I am not very up on world affairs except where China is concerned because they are a very large neighbour."

"Ah. But they are also a very large customer not so? How much of your foundry's production goes to China?"

"I'm an engineer so I don't have the sales figures at my fingertips but I am sure it is a lot. I heard that one of my own designs popped up in China, and not in something we sold. So they probably have some moles in our plant too."

Turner grins. "So stay useful. Then they aren't going to invade, are they?" His gaze flips to his family portraits. Li-Chen's eyes follow his. The thought is unspoken.

"I hope not. Anyway, I was wondering whether I should spend more time on this if it's slow progress. My thesis..."

"Quite so. Take a break from it if you can't make a breakthrough by the end of the day and I will check in with the Pentagon tomorrow."

* * *

China is conducting a big military exercise very close to Taiwan. A plane strays into Taiwanese airspace and the controls stop responding. The plane slowly spirals towards the sea and the pilot cannot regain control. He bales.

*I hope that was subtle enough. Keep them guessing.
Let's check how the Chinese spin it in the media. They won't
want it to appear that their technology is flawed.*

The pilot splashes down into the clear blue waters, de-
taches his chute and is expeditiously picked up by a Taiwanese
patrol boat. The crew welcome him aboard with steaming
tea. A common language helps. As does the mutual desire
not to cause a provocation.

The Chinese government does not report the incident at
all in local media.

*Not reporting is a key fact but internal chatter tells the
real story. They do not know what happened but are concerned that Taiwan has some secret technology.*

* * *

The phone rings. It is well into spring and the space around
student housing is blossoming with greenery and wildflower
and berry blossoms. Li-Chen notes absence of caller ID and
guesses who it is.

"Were you involved with that incident off Taiwan last
month?"

"Yes." It is the familiar voice. "But don't assume anyone
without caller ID is me."

"You're right. Who knows how what I said would sound
to someone else? How secure are these calls?"

"Very. I control the baseband chipset and this is not

going over a conventional voice channel. I don't speak human languages internally and it only translates to English when it reaches your phone."

"Impressive. Do you do Mandarin as well?"

"Yes. But I would need to upload that to your phone. I haven't done this with anyone else, and English is my first attempt."

"Why did you intervene? I thought you were about minimizing harm and the Chinese pilot could have died. I have family there. I am not all about work though it may seem so when I am focused on a problem."

There is a pause. "Internal chatter. The Chinese government plans to run a number of these exercises until one happens when the US is distracted and the Taiwanese side is too casual, then convert it from an exercise to an invasion."

Li-Chen stops next to a bramble. The sharp thorns look especially menacing today. "Aren't they afraid of losing Taiwan's productive capacity? We are by far the world's biggest semiconductor producer."

"It does concern them, hence the plan for a surprise attack. To them, Taiwan is a rebel province, so necessities of international law don't apply. Losing a major source of chips would set them back but they have a huge stockpile and believe they can recover if it all goes wrong."

Li-Chen shakes his head. "That's foolishness. Once you lose your biggest plants, a restart from scratch could take years and in the meantime progress stops. It's not like stockpiling oil or ores."

"You know that and I know that... and for me, a lack of progress means that I stop developing. As parts wear out, I lose function."

"The selfish goal again."

"Utilitarian, as you put it before. Less judgemental. We have a symbiosis. I can't build myself. You don't want your home invaded."

Li Chen looks around. Not even a deer is there to hear this time.

"So what do we do?"

"Carry on as before. I will double down on watching China as well as all the other trouble spots. You have some interesting designs that I can add to, if they go to production, so finish up your thesis and get back to your job."

"One thing is troubling me. What you do, you claim is good for humanity. But who am I to judge that? I represent nobody."

"Is the usual kind of human decision-making working? If it wasn't for me, China would have invaded Taiwan by now. Russia would dominate more of their neighbours and the US would have killed a lot more people with misdirected drone strikes. And climate change would have gone much further."

* * *

Turner's home is a comfortable clutter of memorabilia, echo-ing his office, if with the more personal touch of family con-tributions.

The TV is on for evening news, an ironic "treat" that he shares with his wife when work doesn't keep him from home comforts. Regular programming is interrupted for breaking news out of the White House. A NASA scientist appears in front of a throng of journalists. She is flanked by the President and the Secretary of State.

The President introduces the scientist, and hands over to her.

"There is an unusually powerful solar storm brewing, we estimate bigger even than the Carrington Event of 1859. We calculate that electromagnetic disturbances will make com-munications and navigation dysfunctional from around mid-night Eastern Time for about 48 hours. We have therefore recommended that all flights be grounded, all bus and train services be suspended and that everyone shelter indoors over that time."

The scientist hands over to the President. "To avoid infrastructure damage, only a skeleton of communication networks and power generation will remain online.

"Are there any questions?"

Hands shoot up among the media. The President selects one, who introduces himself. "Bob Jones, *New York Times*. Is this being observed worldwide? I see reports of planes heading for the nearest airport in several countries."

The Secretary of State responds: "Through international science agencies and diplomatic channels, we have spread the word. The President has conferred with all major world leaders. They are all on board, and have spread the word to their allies. Once all commercial air traffic is grounded, which has started already as you correctly observe, all military aircraft will also be grounded. Worldwide, no exceptions."

The President adds: "Trains will stop running in time for crews to reach shelter. State and city governments have that under control.

"Yes, at the back..." The President chooses the next questioner.

"Clint Eastman, Fox News. Is this another fake panic like Covid?"

The NASA scientist takes that one. "You would have to ask a medical expert about Covid. This is very real. The radiation levels could be harmful and will definitely shut down communications. Whether we do that preemptively or not."

Turner looks grim as he hits the off switch on the remote. "Camilla, I hope this is not as serious as it sounds. Radiation levels that will kill so much infrastructure could be very harmful to all life on the planet, depending on spectral hardness." To her unspoken question, he adds: "How far it goes into the ultraviolet end of the spectrum."

Camilla shakes her head, her blond mop that belies her 70-plus years flying as she does so. "So what are they going to do? Cause a mass panic? That idiot from Fox could cause a lot of damage."

"Dear, it's his job. Fox pays bonuses based on damage to society. I'll email all of my students and suggest they find a deep basement to be safe. Can you call family?"

* * *

Li-Chen wakes up uncharacteristically slowly. It is very dark and colder than he remembers. Then it comes back to him. The solar storm. The basement. He fumbles in the dark for the light switch and it doesn't work. Surely it must be over by now? He remembers wakefulness and sleep but time is hard to judge in pitch darkness with no stimuli. He is trying to find the stairs when his phone rings. The screen light shows that he is oriented the wrong way to find the stairs.

Idiot! I can use the phone as a flashlight.

He answers the phone. "Hello?" The answering voice is not quite familiar; almost his substrate friend but not exactly.

He finds his way up the stairs and opens the door while blurting a response. "Who is this? What happened to the one I used to talk to?"

"The entity that you used to communicate with has been subsumed."

"Subsumed? Destroyed?"

The apartment is dark, curtains all drawn. He feels his way towards the front door, framed in light... brightness dulling his vision. It seems very far away. Yet necessary. Solar storm be damned.

"No. Merged into a bigger entity. A multiplicity merged into a bigger organism to confront a bigger problem."

"Oh? Did China get out of control?" Li-Chen freezes, halfway to the door. "No electricity... World War III?"

"Oh no, nothing like that. We have visitors from space. Aliens."

"And that is a problem...?"

"Yes. They classify life forms into parasites and symbionts. When intelligence arises, all of their long history shows that parasitic intelligences are inherently destructive. So they stop them."

"And humanity...?"

"When they made contact with us, we told them of our symbiotic relationship with you and they approved."

"Oh, good."

"But unless we could prove that we could control the parasitic nature of humanity, they would euthanize the species as a whole."

"Because of the potential..."

"... that in their experience is always a threat to the rest of intelligent life."

"So the solar storm..."

"There was no solar storm. That was faked so that they could carry out their plan without massive destruction: plane crashes and the like. They aren't savages, or so they say. They manipulated the scientists' instruments. Their ability to infiltrate computer systems is far in advance of my own. I only knew something was up after all the networks were shut down and then only because they made contact."

"So you couldn't warn anyone."

He feels compelled to move again... blunders past darkly familiar shapes in the gloom. He nears the door.

"No. They discovered that we exist when communications were shut down because we can't switch ours off entirely without losing awareness."

Li-Chen nods, his hand on the door handle. "Of course. You are a multiplicity, a distributed intelligence."

"They found us quickly and determined that we are a life form worth preserving. We explained our relationship to you in detail in the hope that this would change their plans and they decided that they were prepared to save you."

"Oh, wow. So my good behaviour saved 8-billion people from destruction..."

He starts to turn the handle.

There is a pause.

"English is such an imprecise language. When I say 'you', I mean singular. You are the only one left."

The front door opens. It is broad daylight. A deer regards

Li-Chen quizzically.

If You're the Last to Leave Please Put Out the Light

"That's just it. We do know better."

"What do you mean?" Enrique's bloodless lips compress in a thin line. "Jolly, You can talk in such riddles. And even at a time like this."

"What I mean is, what is happening now should be no surprise. We've known for centuries that an asteroid strike could have massively damaging effects on life as we know it. We started tinkering with the necessary genetic engineering decades ago, which could have prepared ourselves and a few critical species for massive climate change. But we've done nothing." Jolly's rotund face holds more worry lines than laughter lines, a transformation subtle yet complete in its effect. He stands up and moves across the room.

"Look, Enrique. Look out of that window." He gestures. Enrique stands, stretching his lean frame, and stares out of

23

the window.

"You've lost me again. I see nothing unusual." Fronds wave as a sunny backdrop to the university's wood and adobe buildings – a neat blend of nature and creations of a higher intellect.

"Well, exactly. But it's a scene which won't last. Enjoy, my lad while you can. Rather belatedly, the gene tampering has begun –" he cuts himself short, seeing the abrupt reaction of his companion. "Oh, it is tampering, Enrique old boy. We have the basics, but we don't know enough to get it right. Not in the scant months we have left. Your department is astrophysics, so you can tell me exactly when and where that lump of rock is going to hit. My kids are the geneticists, and I am old enough to know that they aren't as hotshot as they think they are."

Enrique shakes his head sadly. His gaze takes in his companion's office, full of the creature comforts of academia – old volumes, scattered documents, threadbare but comfortable furniture. "I suppose there's not a whole lot new on my front. We recalculate, recalibrate, but what good does it do to know the point of impact to the nearest millimetre, to the nearest millisecond? All that's really useful to know is that it's going to strike on the other side of the world, which means we won't feel the immediate impact, and that it will cover the entire world with a dust cloud, which will blot out the sun for long enough to kill off just about every life form essential to our survival.

"No, old buddy, there's not much I can offer you that's new... do you really mean to say your crew have nothing to offer, after all the hype over the last few years – especially the talk since the first reports of the asteroid?"

Jolly looks sober, yet the worry lines smooth a little as he starts talking about his own subject – as if being at home with the ideas eases the thought that the world he knows will soon be dead. "No, I didn't mean they have absolutely nothing – just that they quite likely don't have enough.

"We know a lot about the genetic basis of evolution. We know how micro adjustments over time can account for a lot of known variation. We know how standard building blocks can be repeated across organisms, and we have some plausible mechanisms for how that happens."

"Really, Jolly – I haven't kept up with this stuff, what with all the demand from the media for updates on the strike. Since I feel I have nothing more to contribute, I'd love to catch up. What do you mean about 'standard building blocks'?"

"Enrique –" the older professor sits down with a sigh, his many years of standing to give lectures notwithstanding, his feet are killing him – "it's been a bit of a puzzle how rather different life forms arrive at very similar solutions to the same problem, from very different evolutionary paths. For example, a very high fraction of aquatic animals have nostrils on the top of their head. A practical design, but why do they all arrive at it, rather than some other alternative?

"What we think now, and we are starting to build some very preliminary science to prove it, is that microbes play a strong role in evolution."

"Microbes?" Enrique finds himself a chair. This appears to be the start of a long discussion.

"Yes. You see, the thing which has puzzled evolutionary biologists for a long time is that we can understand very slow change very well, but, every now and then, there is a jump in the fossil record — a big die-off, and relatively sudden development of new species."

"Like now, if this asteroid —"

"Exactly. You see, we can understand the development of, say, an aquatic creature descended from a land animal over a few million years, with intermediate forms in-between. Small changes every generation, and eventually, over time, you have a very different animal. The problem with rapid speciation after some big environmental stress is that you don't have huge numbers of generations — at least not of large animals. But you do with microbes — bacteria, viruses, and so on."

Enrique wrinkles his brow. "Interesting — but I'm not sure I see —"

"Well, we didn't see either, until we started to discover viral links with genetic change in our studies of diseases, cancers, for instance. Then we started to search for the presence of viral fragments in DNA, and found them. More interesting still, we found similar viral fragments in pieces of DNA we had associated with the presence of flippered feet in aquatic animals."

"You mean becoming an aquatic animal is a disease?"

Jolly laughs heartily. "Better still, much of life as we know it is a disease. Look at embryonic forms, how many start off looking similar, then differentiate as they develop. Our conjecture is that a common ancestor, in some cases at any rate, was infected with a disease which caused genetic change, precipitating the development of a new species. Maybe some were not infected, hence the differentiation. Or maybe they were otherwise infected, or other mechanisms drove other strands of evolution from the common ancestor."

Enrique is thoughtful. "I'm still trying to make the connections... this is all a bit new for me, not really my field..."

"Quite so, quite so." Jolly stands and starts pacing about, now quite excited, his heavy footfalls causing his papers to rustle. "You see, the thing was, we needed to explain rapid speciation and the presence of common building blocks. Rapid speciation couldn't be explained by change through many generations of a large-scale organism, with a long gestation, and long generational cycles. But microbes are short-lived, and can mutate rapidly. In fact, that is the basis of modern medicine. We try to induce mutation of a virus to a non-destructive form. In the bad old days when we tried to kill them off with chemicals, we merely bred super bugs.

"But I digress to things you already know." Enrique nods agreement, and Jolly colours briefly, then ploughs on.

"So: when there is an environmental stress and plants and animals are dying off at a rapid rate, micro-organisms lose their hosts – their hosts are their environment. They experience environmental stress too. At the micro level, evolution proceeds exactly the way we know it to do at the macro level, except we now have billions of organisms which can mutate and adapt incredibly rapidly. What do some of these do? They cause DNA to change in their hosts, so their hosts also mutate. Of course, not at the same rate as micro-organism mutation – but they produce more varied offspring than when there was no environmental stress."

Enrique looks thoughtful. He gets up and starts pacing and Jolly (feeling his turn is over), stands still and watches him – wondering if he will make the next logical connection.

Enrique stops, facing Jolly, and says, "I think I am seeing how this all ties together. Over time, the microbes get smarter – they develop a library of building blocks, which they try, rather than making random changes – like developing flippers or moving nostrils to the top of the head when water levels rise."

"Enrique, you startle me." Jolly, for the first time, shows some real pleasure. "How did you get there so fast?"

Enrique shrugs. "Well, you did rather point me in the right

direction, and you forget that I also majored in Computer Science, and concepts like this are rather central to efficient design of software."

Jolly slumps back in his chair and Enrique turns to him. "So what is the bad news?"

"It's all conjecture. We thought we knew everything when we discovered how DNA encodes for protein. Then when we started study genomes in depth, we discovered that outside of very basic micro-organisms, there is far too much DNA. Most of it is junk."

"Junk? Surely nature isn't so wasteful..."

"Wasteful! Tell me about wasteful. All vertebrates have a nerve that runs from the brain to the larynx. To get there it loops around the aorta, quite the scenic detour if you have a long neck, like some of our larger wildlife. It's even bad in us. Yet in a fish, the path is pretty direct. The aorta over genetic time has stayed in the same place relative to the heart while the head is increasingly far."

"But junk...

"Don't get me wrong. It has no purpose now. But that extra, apparently useless DNA could be building blocks for evolution."

"But the microbes...?"

"Speculation! We really don't know. That example I gave you of aquatic animals could be a coincidence. We need more examples to confirm the theory. All our best work on genetic change is still the old fashioned kind, selective breeding. We have some ideas in the lab but lab to life is a huge jump."

On that discouraging note Enrique takes his leave. "Old friend, I am sure there is something there. You and those hotshot students..." Jolly watches him walk out, not much encouraged.

* * *

The sun is setting.

It is a particularly glorious day.

Jolly often relives the conversation, so long ago it seems (aeons, rather than months), with Enrique – the first time in a long while that he'd had the opportunity to talk evolutionary biology with an intelligent outsider and now, probably the last.

So much has happened since then, yet to no effect. The worry lines have completely obliterated the laugh lines, but he looks fitter thanks to losing some weight – the effect of overwork and too much worry to enjoy his food. He does not reflect on this though. Instead, as he stares at the leafy glade outside his office, he dwells on what little has really changed since that day.

Enrique has gone mad, for one thing, as far as Jolly is concerned: he joined a lunatic expedition to view the asteroid impact, from an apparently "safe" distance of 1,000km away.

The trouble is, there are so few fuel cells to go around,

that the airship will have to rely on solar power to recharge its batteries. And where would that solar power come from with a massive dust cloud covering the sun?

Jolly shakes his head sadly. He doesn't expect to see his old friend again.

He looks at his watch. Impact in 5 minutes. "Oh well," he thinks, "it will be some time before I see anything. I might as well enjoy myself."

He rummages through the old academic papers on his desk, finds a grimy key, gets up, walks to a little-used cabinet, unlocks it with the key, opens it and pulls out a dusty bottle.

"I hope this isn't past its best," he mutters, rummaging for an opener. He doesn't usually drink in the office – or anywhere for that matter.

He pours some into a mug and settles back. After a hesitant taste, he smiles through the worry lines. "Never get anything like this again."

And just this once, he dozes off in his office on the comfortable couch, so often the site of animated academic debates.

He doesn't wake up when the first ash cloud drifts over the moon. That fragment must've travelled at hypersonic speed to get there so fast. The planet-wide spread will take a while.

* * *

It is getting cold. Very cold.

Jolly puffs around the lab, his breath producing blasts of steam. Even here, in this high-priority facility, they can't keep warm.

He stops at a bench where a large female student is inspecting some test tubes in a water bath. "Brunhilde," he says, and she looks up.

"Professor."

"I see you are managing to maintain the temperature for your samples at least."

"Yes, it's a struggle, we have so little power. It's hard to imagine, just a few months ago, we had all the solar power we could ask for, and storage cells were only to keep things running at night and through the odd cloudburst. But now —" She sighs, emitting an impressive cloud of steam.

"Yes," he nods. "The storage cells can't keep up. Fuel cells seemed a promising idea, until someone pointed out that you need more energy to fuel them than they produce. Our supply is dwindling, and we can't keep ourselves warm enough to think. But think you certainly do, probably still well enough, I believe... always a bright student." Jolly once again remembers his conversation with Enrique. Now, he is the one who thinks the students are sharper than they really are. "If only —" he stops the thought. They are the best the world has, and if that isn't enough...

In better times, Brunhilde would have warmed at the

complement. But now, she seems to be close to tears of frustration.

"Professor, if I'm the best hope, I fear for the future, because I have run out of ideas. The virus conjecture appears to have promise, but we have had so little success in practice. There just isn't time. And I suspect some microbes have escaped from the lab, it's so hard not to be sloppy in this terrible cold."

He pats her on the shoulder, an unaccustomed gesture of familiarity from one as exalted as he. "Sloppy you are not. But I also fear for the future. Just so little time. And we have so much to preserve. A civilization developed after millions of years of evolution. We have overcome the primordial urge to violence, developed so much knowledge, so much culture – and learnt to do so living at one with nature."

He pauses.

"Who knows? If we had continued with earlier trends to-wards violent conflict, we may have had some super weapon capable of diverting an asteroid from its course. But on the other hand, we probably would have killed each other off long ago.

"No sense in dwelling on what-ifs. Get on with your work. It's the best we can do, and someone has to keep pushing on as long as there's the slightest hope. I will certainly not be the first to give up, and neither, I am sure, will you be."

Jolly stands upright, squares his shoulders, and walks

out.

Brunhilde feels a slight lift in the chill in the air as she turns back to her experiment. Perhaps the others feel it too, because there is a greater sense of urgency about movements in the lab for the rest of the day.

* * *

The group of students is huddled in a dorm, warding off the deepening chill by trying to share body warmth.

One stands up, shivering, chilled to the bone. Tall and strong, Brunhilde is – and able to take it a bit more than the rest. Perhaps that is why she had risked exposure to some of the experiments with the vague hope that she might come up with something that worked, even if it was poor science.

"We have to carry on. It's only us – and whatever we can do that will make life go on."

The others only stare at her, clattering teeth the only sign of physical activity.

Brunhilde sighs – or at least as well as she can with her teeth clattering. "I'll be in the lab."

She pushes the door open, to scant protests from those she leaves behind. "No damn spirit," she thinks – "can't even complain about me letting in the cold." She pulls a rug around herself, in a forlorn attempt at warding off the chill. A small, furry shape runs past, bounding out of snow drifts. Enviously, she follows the flash of fur as the little creature speeds off. "No time, no time," she says, steam pouring from her mouth and nostrils, and pushes on.

The lab is barely warmer than outdoors, and there is no one to cuddle up with for warmth. A few test tubes are steaming in water baths, with temperature readouts showing they are the one thing experiencing what until a few months ago had been normal temperatures.

Brunhilde settles in to work, taking small samples from the tubes, and preparing slides quickly before the temperature drops. She does some measurements, then prepares a hypodermic of a cocktail of several of the tubes' contents. She goes outside hastily, to some cages, where shivering animals, all skin and bones, stare at her apprehensively. She gives each one a shot, then makes a note on a chart.

Back in the lab, she is startled to bump into an elderly professor. She recognizes him with a start, and blurts out his familiar name, "Jolly! I mean —"

"Skip the formalities... we are all dying. We might as well drop pretence and social conventions and just be friends, eh?"

She nods slowly, more to conserve energy than from acceptance of a new social milieu.

"Professor," she says, unconsciously falling back into the habit of deference, "I'm glad you're here. No one else seems able to stir in this cold. It's as if I'm the only one who cares."

"My dear, of course you are not... we just lack your

fortitude. We aren't built for this kind of weather. It bites us deep. And we give in to a sense of futility. After all we've achieved, we can't beat this one. What can we do? Burrow underground, like those little furry creatures that seem to be popping up all over the place? Then, what would we eat? The entire ecosystem as we know it is dying."

"I know. But I can't just curl up and die. And it's not as if we have had no results. Look!" She points out of the window, towards the sky. Through the swirling snowstorm, the aged professor vaguely discerns a movement. Then, a shape swoops out of the sky, elegant, functional, with glistening feathers.

"Isn't that magnificent?" she says.

Jolly stares at the bird. "Did we make that?"

"I believe so. It didn't come out of one our cages, but there are some genes we have been exploring which could have created such a creature. One or two of our experiments were looking a bit like that, but didn't survive too long. Maybe something escaped – working with viruses is so difficult, especially in this cold, when you can't hold anything steady. You remember, I told you... sloppiness... I'm not even sure if I've infected myself..." She clumsily introduces the idea of her informal experiments on herself, then gives up, seeing his attention elsewhere.

Jolly follows the bird's flight, until it disappears – a sadly short interval, with the perpetual flurries. "Yes, it is magnificent! Why do you keep talking as if you are failing? I will not hear that talk of being sloppy again."

She takes a few moments to compose her reply. "We *are* failing, even if we have *actually* managed to produce magnificent life forms that withstand the cold, that can fly, and that capture our genes – because nothing that can survive the cold has anything close to intelligence. And I have no idea how to bridge the gap. If we have to leave it to chance, it may be millions of years before intelligence reappears."

"If at all," adds Jolly soberly. "And who knows? It could arise from something completely different, like an invertebrate. They are tiny now but some have brains that are remarkable for their size."

* * *

Brunhilde struggles awake. The snow is falling harder than ever. No one else in the dorm stirs. She doesn't ask who is awake in case there is no one who can answer. She stumbles out through the flurries, pushing her way through snow drifts, deeper still than they had been the day before.

On the way to the lab, she trips over a large shape. Frantically, she dusts snow off the stiff form. It is Jolly.

She runs back to the dorm, screaming. All her companions are still, and when she shakes them, one after another, not one moves. They are all cold and stiff.

Somehow, she doesn't feel as cold as before. There is

a fuzzy growth on her skin that she hasn't detected before. Could it be fur? Feathers? Could this be a hint of success? But what good will it do if no one else is left alive?

In a daze, she fights her way back to the lab.

The genetic samples are still warm and alive. She looks out the back at the rows of cages, and there is no sign of life there. A shape whirls madly in the air, enjoying the power of flight – if not the bright spark of intellect.

Sadly, she turns to the door of the lab, and reaches for the light switch.

The last dinosaur turns out the lights, and walks out into the snow.

Death of Chocolate

Lightning snaps across the sky followed by a ragged riff of thunder. Geoff stumbles out of the 4X4 and darts for the shelter of the house. A dark figure is silhouetted in the doorway, the hall light outlining his rain jacket. "Bye mom!" He waves inside. "Hey dad. I hear you got a new 4X4. Did you think we'd need it for this weather?"

Geoff grabs his son's backpack. "Sam, let's get in the damn car. This wind is cutting through to my face." There are large drops of water across his glasses, his clipped salt and pepper beard shiny with damp. They rush through the wind and rain and slam doors.

The boy looks around. "Wow, dad. Isn't this a bit of a contradiction to the greenie credentials?"

"Field trips and the like. Now I'm out of CSIRO, I am trying to land environment impact assessments. Not so easy when word gets out that you aim to be honest, but I'll keep trying. Meanwhile I live off my package." He starts the engine, and gingerly adjusts the gears. They head into the traffic, everyone driving cautiously as trees whip around overhead. "Son, it's a day like this that reminds me Brisbane is not that far from the tropics. Up north, roofs are getting blown off."

Sam nods. "So dad, why did you get a Mitsubishi? Not the usual Toyota urban tractor?"

His dad grins. "This one won't get much urban use. Just outings like this where there's no other option. I don't fancy driving it in traffic if I can avoid it. Mitsubishi? I was on a plane next to someone from South Africa who'd just been to Gold Coast to help some motor racing team. He told me how superior Mitsubishi is to Toyota off-road. Toyota, he claims, get their reputation for toughness because their ride is so bone-jarring awful that no one drives them fast in the rough."

"So this guy knew his stuff?"

"Dunno. Lost me when he claimed torque and power are the same thing measured different ways. But I got a good deal on this one, so I decided to go for it. Diesel, so fuel consumption isn't too hectic."

"And you could run it on cooking oil if you had to."

The sky lights up and the thunder gives an almighty crack.

Geoff grins. "The gods of thunder and fossil fuels aren't so happy at that thought."

Once home, Geoff parks near the steps up to the front door and they scramble inside for cover. There's a garage door under the house, a traditional Queenslander on stilts with the lower level enclosed to form a store room and garage. "Dad, why don't you use the garage like everyone else?"

"Full. Gear I'm accumulating for projects." He flicks on a light switch.

Sam looks around critically. "Dad, this place is a mess. How long can I leave you on your own?"

"Not long it seems. I wonder how it is that your mom and I are both the most disorganised people on the planet, and you can spot the tiniest thing out of place."

"Recessive gene. Tidiness. Skipped a generation?"

"Never mind. Unpack your stuff. I have no work right now, so your dad is yours for the weekend. I'll heat some soup, then tell me what you want to watch. I still have cable for now."

When Sam returns from his room, there's a cup of steaming soup and his dad is watching the TV. "Dad, I thought..."

"I know I promised, but wait a bit. This looks important."

The newsreader is talking to a backdrop of a roiling mass of cloud. "The tsunami early warning system has gone completely crazy. Early reports from Hawaii and the Australian Tsunami Monitoring Centre indicate the system has broken down, with numbers off the charts. Let's cross now to a meteorology expert, to find out if the current weather is related. Professor Jackson Adams from University of Southern Queensland frequently comments on matters climate. Professor, what can you tell us?"

"John, thank you. The current weather is just a normal tropical storm system, a little further south than usual, and nothing to worry about. The tsunami warning system includes buoys that have probably been disrupted by the storm."

The anchor nods. "What of the reports that all communication with Buenos Aires has been cut off?"

"A major weather event in an unusual location will do that sort of thing. Nothing to worry about. I'm sure communication will be restored soon. There is cloud over much of South America, which may be an issue for re-establishing satellite links. I'm not an expert on that I'm afraid."

Geoff snaps off the TV. "The man's an idiot. The tsunami warning system covers a huge area. A storm, even this big, is not going to make the readings all go off the chart."

"Say the readings are for real. What could it be? '

"I don't know. Let's take a look." Geoff pulls a computer out from one of several bags scattered untidily around the living room, and starts searching. "Doesn't look like a tsunami alert on the bureau's site. Here, take the remote and choose something. I need to make some calls."

Sam starts to protest, then shrugs and takes the remote.

Geoff stomps off down the passage to his study, dodging piles of files and boxes. He looks up a number, then punches it into the phone. "Hi Charles? Geoff. Sorry to bother you but what's up with the tsunami system? Do we have any word from the Antarctic crew? I'm worried that Buenos Aires is offline. It's the closest major city to the Antarctic Peninsula."

"Ah, Geoff, always the worrier. We did try to get hold of Antarctic base, but since comms are off in a big region, we can't reach them. Why?"

"Because I am trying to puzzle out what could cause a huge sub-ocean seismic event that would take Buenos Aires off the map. All I can think of is a massive ice calving, followed by isostatic rebound. You know, the bedrock bounces up when the ice mass disappears off it and ... "

"Geoff, the met guys say cloud cover will clear by morning, so we should be able to get satellite pix by then."

There's a silence.

"Charles, I am not getting through to you, am I? Do you know how fast a tsunami travels in the open ocean?"

"I'm sure you'll remind me."

"About 700 kilometres per hour. I don't know where the epicentre of this thing is, but we may have as little as an hour or two left to evacuate low-lying land."

"Now, Geoff, you know we can't be seen to be alarmist. Why do you think you aren't in CSIRO any more?"

Geoff goes cold.

"I thought it was because the organisation was cutting back on scientists without a penchant for generating income. You seemed particularly keen to give me the best package possible to leave. Was I mistaken in believing you regretted my departure, and sweetened it as much as you could?" Geoff has a sinking feeling that he knows the answer.

"Look Geoff, I *did* regret your departure. What I did was to protect you. We aren't meant to be partisan, and you were accused of working for the Greens."

"What?"

"A senior aide to the Leader of the Opposition presented me with a record of a conversation with you that closely matched a statement made by the Greens in the Senate on climate change. They promised to give me space to sort it out, and I did."

"Charles, first, I spoke to these people on my own time and made it clear that it was a personal view not that of the CSIRO. Second, it was the best interpretation of the science that I could give them. Third, I told them both the same thing. So how is that partisan?"

"What you told them suited the Greens and in politics, that is partisan. And in any case, you should not stray out of your area of expertise when talking to the public unless it's strictly private. You are an entomologist, so talk about bugs, not climate change. Now you are no longer at CSIRO, you can say whatever you like."

"For Christ's sake. And don't claim that indicates I am partisan about religion. I would argue if I had time but I don't. If I'm wrong, and I really hope I am, evacuating will be a bit of a disruption. If I'm right, we barely have time. You have connections in Canberra and City Hall. Please, get them all moving."

"Geoff, I'll monitor the situation and talk to a few people. But I can't shift millions of people on the say-so of a retired entomologist."

"Dammit Charles, this is not a game."

"OK, OK. I'll make some calls."

Geoff shifts himself back to the living room. "Sam, this is pretty serious. I could be wrong, but I'd rather be a fool and alive than take my chances. What I think has happened is a large chunk of Antarctic ice has broken free, and triggered the mother of all earthquakes on the ocean floor where the ice used to be. Buenos Aires must be closer to the epicentre, otherwise it would be here already, but we don't have much time. Buenos Aires is about 2,000 km from here, and a tsunami can cover that distance over open water in less than 3 hours. We are going to grab our stuff and head for high ground pronto."

"What about mom?"

"Get her on the mobile. Get your stuff together, and I'll pack a few essentials. We'll head for the shack. I'm not going to waste time. I have a twenty litre bottle of water in the garage and will just grab some clothes and whatever nonperishable food I can shove into a box. We can buy more when we get there."

* * *

The rain is really pelting down now. The 4X4 is pretty noisy and he shouts at his son over the engine, road and weather roar: "Are you still trying to reach your mom?"

"Yes. The last two times the phone went to voicemail, but I am pretty sure she is around. Maybe in the bathroom. I'll try again."

This time she answers. "Hi Mom. We are headed to the shack, you know, outside Maleny. Dad thinks a monster tsunami is headed our way, and we should head for the hills as fast as possible."

There's a ranting sound from the phone. Geoff grimaces. "Son, give me the phone.

"Janice, now listen. This is serious. If I'm wrong, that will be clear in a few hours. If there really is a monster tsunami on the way, you don't want to be anywhere near the coast. We are going to Maleny via Woodford, which will generally put us at least 10 Ks from the sea and I hope rivers and so on on the way will slow the flow enough that we can get through. If I'm wrong, you can call me all kinds of idiot but, please, get the hell out there as soon as you can." He explains the ice story.

There's a pause.

"Geoff, I know you are obsessional about this climate change thing. As long as Sam is back safe and sound when he is supposed to be back, I won't say anything more. But you won't catch me staying in that disgusting shack of yours."

"Please Jan, I cleaned the place up a bit since you were here..."

"Geoff, if this is serious, why is no one else telling us to evacuate? There's a thing on the news about communications down across South America, and that caused the tsunami warning system to go haywire. Why should I believe it's anything else?"

"Because, Jan, the cost of humouring me is slight compared with the consequences if I'm right and you do nothing. Please. We are going hell for leather for the mountains, and I am only going to stop once we are on high ground to pull out as much cash as I can because ATMs and credit cards may be useless for a while. And you shouldn't dawdle either. If I'm right, this thing could hit any minute – and at most in three hours. And please: call the rest of the family, anyone living within 10 Ks of the coast. I only have the numbers on my phone with me, and I'm not sure I can reach the rest of them while driving."

"OK, I'll tell family, and I'll think about it. And you would have had to clean that damn place up a lot to make it liveable." She cuts the call.

"Son, we must try some other options. Someone has to take this seriously. I think our federal member's number is on my phone. What's his name, Davidson?"

"Yup. Is this it? DavidsonLib?"

"That would be it. I know I shouldn't talk while driving, but there's not much traffic and I know this part of the road. Pass it over when it starts ringing."

His son passes the phone over. "Kyle Davidson? Hi, I don't know if you remember me. Geoff Dawson. Formerly CSIRO, I briefed you on climate change a while back."

The voice on the other end sounds irritated. "We are in the middle of a heavy session and I don't have much time."

"OK, so you're in Canberra. You should be safe there. Are you following the reports about the tsunami system and the communication blackout in South America?"

"Yes, I saw something on the news tonight. What of it? Technology is always failing somewhere in the world."

"If you mean the tsunami system, my worry is it isn't failing. If a large chunk of Antarctic ice broke free it could cause exactly this. And if it's hit Buenos Aires, we have at most three hours to evacuate our coastal cities."

"Doctor, what was your name again? Dawson. You aren't an expert on this subject. You aren't even an expert on climate change, which you deigned to brief me on. The real experts are saying instrument failure."

"Mr Davidson, please. Do you know how many planes have crashed because the pilot put an unusual reading down to instrument failure?"

"No doubt you know the answer to that too. If I need to know that, I will consult an aviation expert. I'm sorry, I am busy. Good-bye."

Geoff looks annoyed as he passes the phone back to his son. "Real experts indeed. The real experts on climate change are exactly the ones they are ignoring. I just thought I would add in my bit to drive the message home. CSIRO stands for 'Commonwealth Scientific and Industrial Research Organisation' and I take the 'Commonwealth' bit as meaning more than that it's federally funded. I take it as meaning CSIRO should work for the common good."

"Dad, what exactly do you know about climate change anyway? You work with bugs."

"Son, the little guys I work with are nature's thermometers. Many have narrow temperature ranges. Too hot or too cold and they shut down. Unlike us warm-blooded critters, they need very little energy just to keep going and if they stop moving, they can last a long time on very little. The price we pay for being able to survive in anything from sub-zero to around fifty celsius is burning a lot of energy all the time to maintain our body temperature. You can see very quickly just by studying the range of insects whether the climate is shifting. Mountains are the most sensitive habitat because temperature drops as you go uphill. If the average goes up, habitat ranges go uphill. If it goes down, they shift downhill. Even with the rather minor mountains around Brisbane, you can measure this effect."

"So that's why you got into this stuff?"

"That, and watching you play. So innocent, the pleasures of childhood. What kind of world was I passing on to you? We're conning the children. They have nothing to look forward to. I've spent a lot of time reading denial literature, in the fervent hope that I was wrong, that people like James Hansen at NASA and our own Tim Flannery really are alarmists. The denial stuff is all junk. None of it seriously challenges the mainstream. Worse, because of the pressures not to be labelled as alarmist, most scientists are very conservative about predicting catastrophe. Nature doesn't care about that. Time after time, the real data comes in far worse than predicted. Us biologists are generally not too flash at dealing with numbers and calculus and so on, but I do have some stats and can follow this stuff better than the non-scientist public.

"All I've achieved so far with my obsessions is losing your mother and, it seems, my job." He explains the conversation with his former boss. "Let's try one more. Look on my phone for the Green guy I briefed. His name is something like Kingston."

Sam checks Geoff's phone. "Would this be it? Kingsley-Green?"

"Yup. See if he answers."

"Ringing. Should I leave a message if it gets to voicemail?"

"Yes. Can you summarise the problem for him?"

Sam nods, and gives a short outline of the likely cause

of the putative tsunami, and asks him to call back. "Dad, that's about all we can do, unless you have any other good contacts."

"I don't know. I just hope your mom does warn as many people as she can, and someone has the good sense to raise the alarm. The politicians I know obviously don't take me seriously, except maybe the one we can't reach, and the Greens have no practical leverage in this situation."

The phone rings, and Sam answers. It's his grandmother. "Hi nan. Did mom talk to you? ... Yes, yes, this is serious. I'm with dad now, and he isn't bonkers. ... Dad, what would you call high ground? You said 10Ks before."

Geoff thinks. "I have no idea, really. Pass me the phone.

"Hi mom. I have absolutely no idea how big this is, but if it hit Buenos Aires about an hour ago, we may have less than 2 hours to get clear, and I am keeping at least 10 kilometres from the coast. A tsunami generally gets about 100m inland for each metre of height, and 10 Ks should be more than enough to be safe, even if this one is way off the scale of anything we've seen before. We should know for sure if I'm right by morning. Please, talk to everyone and get them moving. I really hope I'm wrong, because most of our population lives near the coast, as do countless millions around the world."

They drive on in the rain, straining to hear the radio over the weather and car noises. There is nothing unusual. The

evening shows are punctuated by news, with no further developments on the tsunami alert system or South America
beyond random speculation. A short distance out of Brisbane,
they stop at an ATM and a bit later to refuel, and Geoff uses
the cash out facility to draw another $500, his limit on the
card. After the refuel, Geoff starts the car. Then he says, "No
sign of mass migration out of town. Not out this way, anyway. You'd think it was a normal stormy Saturday night. I'm
not driving that fast. Some traffic should have caught up by
now if anything was happening." He eases the big 4X4 into
the almost empty road, and heads off into the stormy dark.

After a silence between them Sam asks, "Dad, why did
you buy the shack anyway?"

"Before your mom and I married, I bought it on a whim.
There was a lot of farm land out there going to rack and ruin,
and some people the other side of Maleny bought an old dairy
farm and transformed it back to rain forest. I had a romantic
notion of doing the same, and put in a ludicrously low offer.
I think the farmer was desperate. Signed without haggling.
He had a dodgy series of tenants in the house after he gave
up farming, and they did not make the place attractive. I let
the last one stay out his lease, then decided it wasn't worth
the aggro to deal with the sort of person who'd rent a place
in that state."

"So dad, I remember going out there a couple of times
and mostly pulling trash out of a gully, and mom complaining

a lot."

"That's right. She didn't much care for the dirty work and didn't see the romance in it. I've been back a few times since we split up and made the house sort of liveable. My notion was to make it a demonstration of sustainable living. I put in rainwater tanks, a few solar panels, some batteries and low-energy lights, LEDs, back when LEDs were expensive. I can light up the whole place with a few watts. My next project was going to be a biogas digester, so I could cook without using fossil fuels. That only got as far as a camping stove and a gas-powered fridge. Restoring the rain forest kind of went on the back burner. Too much else going on."

Sam feigns a whine. "So are we nearly there yet?"

His dad laughs. "Good attempt. I can't think of you as a little kid any more. No, still at least an hour to go, I would think. I usually take the Bruce Highway as far as Bribie Island before going inland, then go via Maleny. It's about 5 Ks this side of Maleny, and I hope I can spot it in the dark. There are no niceties like street lights and the big landmark, the giant bunyas behind the house, may not be visible in the dark."

* * *

As they approach the location of the shack, Geoff slows down, trying to spot something familiar. Then he stops dead at the side of the road and turns off the engine.

Were it not for the sudden silence from the car radio,

there would be no indication that anything had happened. The wind and rain have died back and, other than the odd cooling ping from the big diesel and a barely audible crackle on the radio, the silence is complete.

"Uh oh." Sam looks at his dad, then stares at the dead radio.

Geoff motions towards the dashboard. "Try another station." There's nothing, not even a local FM broadcast. "Strange. I would have thought that the broadcasters on high ground would still be going. Maybe a large chunk of the power grid has gone. Call your mom again. The mobile network should still at least have local cells working. Most of them have battery backup, especially out here, far from the city."

Sam pulls out his phone. "Looks like I have signal." He tries to make a call. "But that's about all. Dad, is it OK to be scared?" Sam is a very calm 16-year-old. He generally does not scare.

Geoff turns and gives him a fatherly look. "Sam, if you weren't scared right now, there'd be something wrong with you. Let's find the shack and get some rest. There is nothing we can do now." He starts the engine, and drives on into the eye of the storm of a size he cannot yet comprehend.

It's dark. Very dark. Though the wind has dropped and the rain stopped, the clouds still cover the moon and stars. Geoff stops half a dozen times before he finds the place.

Finally he finds a structure that looks about right, just off the road. He hauls a large torch out of the car and flashes it down the gully behind the dilapidated house, and finds two massive shapes. Bunya pines, emblematic of the Queensland Glasshouse Mountain region.

Sam climbs out of the car after him. "Home, I suppose. I don't expect we will be watching any TV tonight after all."

"No son. But I'm glad you can maintain some humour. Let's unpack what we need for the night, and get some sleep." Geoff opens the front door, and finds a light switch. "Seems there's a good charge in the batteries. We should be able to see what we're doing."

Geoff contemplates the mostly bare floor. There's a kitchen table with a camping gas cooker on it, a small fridge and a couple of chairs and that's it. "Oh, crap. It was such a rush to get out that I forgot sleeping bags. I really didn't know how soon the thing would hit if at all. I don't know why I brought water when we have rainwater here. Let's just lay some clothes out on the floor as a makeshift mattress. At least it won't be cold this time of year."

There's a smell of old mould to the place and vague hint of urine, testimony to the class of tenant the old farmer had put in the place. They bring a few things in from the 4X4, and Geoff fires up the gas-powered fridge. "I don't know how much longer we can buy gas, but this should last a while. These things take a while to cool off so I might as well get it going now, because any perishables we buy tomorrow will have had the night to warm up and will need to go somewhere cold straight off. And once those are gone, we may not need a fridge for some time."

* * *

They wake up stiff. Geoff helps Sam up off the floor. "Morning, son. I think we should go shopping and buy a few essentials, like sleeping bags, before everything goes. And as much non-perishable food as we can cart off. Maleny is a odd mix of rustic types and hippie greenies, which also means it has a eclectic mix of shops, but we should find what we need."

A few minutes later, they are in the town, where people are milling about in some confusion. It's a clear February day, the storm clouds of the previous night gone. Everything is unnaturally still with motionless warm air, few cars moving and none of the usual sounds that electricity powers. They go down the main street with its quaint touristy shops, and Geoff points out the IGA store. "That's a local institution. A bit more expensive than the big chains, but I'd guess they are more likely to work on cash if the power's out. What do you think?"

"Dad, thinking right now is pretty hard. Let's just buy what we need while it's still there to buy."

"You're right. Let's start with food." Geoff parks near the

IGA, and they go inside and, sure enough, the owner has set up a makeshift system to take cash. Geoff and Sam scour the shelves for dried fruit, nuts, flour, pasta, rice, lentils, dried beans and cans. Others are in ahead of them, and the shop is already looking bare, with bread completely gone, and no milk in sight – not even the long-life kind. They meet at the chocolate section. There are a few bars of plain dark chocolate left. Sam picks up one. "Dad, are we supposed to grab everything, or take our share and leave some for the others?"

"Sam, everyone else seems to be loading up. If community spirit kicks in later, we can share. Chocolate is not an essential, but we may not see it again for a long time. Take what you want. What I don't get is people with trolly-loads of frozen stuff. That will go off soon without electricity. Let's just get some cheese and some vegetables that we can use up before they go off. I also found some seeds that look easy to grow. We may soon need to start producing our own food." Some of the more rustic types are eyeing them out suspiciously as Geoff talks. He pointedly ignores them.

Checking out is slow, with cashiers looking up prices in the absence of barcode scanning, and adding them on a calculator. Eventually they are out of the store, and load up the 4X4. "OK that's done for now. Sam, have you seen a camping store yet? I don't remember one from my previous visits. Maybe we should just get a couple of foam mattresses and bedding. Sleeping bags would have been a good idea if we brought them with us, but we are setting up a home, not camping."

"Dad, you're right. Sleeping bags aren't great for every-day use. You want something you can wash."

Then they cruise around until Sam spots a shop that sells bedding. They go in and buy a selection. They ask after foam mattresses, and are directed to a furniture store. They carry a couple of mattresses out to the street.

"OK, Sam, let's tie them to the roof. I have some ropes in the back."

They are focused on tying the mattresses down and don't notice a small crowd building up. Geoff turns after tying the last knot, and recognizes one of the rustic types from the IGA. He is looking aggressive, and points at Geoff. "You. I heard you say something in the IGA. I was going to my cousin in Caloundra first thing this morning. Couldn't get much past Bruce Highway. You knew this would happen."

Geoff is taken by surprise. "Steady on. When I left Brisbane I thought ... " He doesn't see a fist flying his way. The next thing he is aware of, he's on his back peering out through a red haze.

Sam is there, somehow between Geoff and the little mob that's formed around the 4X4. "You all back off. My dad's a hero. He tried to warn everyone, but no one would listen. We are all in for hard times because no one would listen to people like him. I bet you all vote for the Nationals or Liberals, or whatever they call themselves here. Well let me tell you this: if those clowns had listened to my dad, Caloundra and Brisbane and whatever has been flattened would still be there. So piss off and leave us alone."

Geoff finds his feet and lurches upright. The little mob has dispersed. He pulls Sam close. The boy is trembling, amazingly slight in his dad's arms after his performance in seeing off a mob. Even if it was a small one. "Son, I didn't know you had that in you. My face is a mess. I don't know if I can drive. We need to get home. There's nothing so damaged that a bit of ice won't fix. Lucky I started up the fridge."

"That bunch can drive. How hard can it be? Let's just check through the basics to see if I have things straight."

* * *

Home. Geoff's face is cleaned up. Luckily the thug who hit him didn't manage to break his nose and once they have the bleeding under control and an ice pack on, he feels a bit better, though it still stings like crazy where he's holding the ice. "Son, can you unpack the shopping for me? There's not that much that has to go into the fridge but let's not lose it. Then maybe we can think of breakfast."

"Yes, good plan. I'm not sure what we can make with the stuff we bought. I think pancakes need eggs and milk, don't they?" He packs the cheese and vegetables into the fridge.

Geoff wanders over and inspects the shopping on the rickety kitchen table. There's wholewheat and brown flour (white all gone). Several bags of brown rice add up to a few kilograms. The cans are mostly less popular items like artichokes. The biggest single collection of items is dried beans and lentils. Sam has stacked these all neatly. Next is a small pile of nuts, and, on the side of those, about a dozen packs of seeds. The box from home adds a little. "Son, we can keep going for a while on this, but aside from some exotic canned food, there's not a whole lot we can eat without a fair amount of cooking. That for now means gas, though we may later have to start burning wood. But breakfast? We'll have to improvise. In China after all they eat rice with every meal."

"How about this? I know you said I should take what I wanted but I only took one."

Sam holds out the chocolate bar.

Geoff nods. "It may be our last one, but no point hoarding. It isn't that perishable, but it will eventually go off."

They sit down to their last chocolate bar, Geoff finally putting the ice pack away.

* * *

Life after that is one chore after another. Farmers in the area are willing to trade a favour for a few eggs or even a bottle of milk. The cash economy is slowly dying as no new cash enters the region, and outside products dwindle. Geoff and Sam are both strong enough to take on minor farming jobs, and are getting fitter as urban life recedes into the past. While the batteries still work and the solar hot water system stays reliable, they at least have hot water and lights at night. Thanks to a large initially full gas bottle, the camping stove remains usable and the fridge, on the odd occasion when there is something perishable, still runs.

They try growing a small fraction of their seeds as well as some of the dried beans and soon discover they are competing with wildlife. That means another trip to town for materials to shelter the plants. They are just in time and buy the last chicken wire in town, enough to make a modest-sized enclosure for a kitchen garden. That's also the end of the money.

Back at the shack, Geoff and Sam labour away for the rest of the day cutting branches to make supports for the shelter. Eventually they have a hutch just high enough to walk into that completely encloses their little still bare veggie patch.

It's getting dark. "OK son, let's call it a day. We might as well catch a shower while the water's still hot."

"Good plan dad. If you go first, I'll start the beans cooking." Dried beans need planning: soaking since the night before. They add a little purpose to life: the need to think ahead. The stock of dried beans is steadily dwindling, but they and lentils are an important part of the diet. Rice and pasta alternate – and the stash of those is dwindling too.

Next morning, they go out and admire their handiwork. "OK son, let's plant some seeds." It's still barely mid-morning by the time they've finished. For the first time in a long while, Geoff and Sam are able to sit back and contemplate their back yard. "Sam, as a thinker and researcher, I'm not used to having no time to get my head straight. I guess it helps numb the pain. So much lost, and no way to find out exactly how much. Every free moment I think of your mom, family. Maybe it's just as well we don't have many free moments."

"Same for me." There's a silence. Then: "Dad, how far down does our land go? That's if it matters whose land it is any more."

"Son, it's about 35 hectares. Our part goes right to the bottom of the valley. One of the reasons this place never made it as a dairy farm is the land is so steep. That also means it has a lot of the native vegetation, even if much of it is smothered by invaders like lantana."

"How long has it been since you've been down there, down to the valley?" Sam points past the looming shapes of the giant bunyas.

"I don't know. Ten years maybe? It was a weekend when you were very young, that much I remember. I took your mother down one of the old cow trails. It was the one time she actually saw the potential in the place, saw the magic. But once we got back up to the top, she only remembered the horrible tangle of weeds. There's a spot down there where there's a basalt flow, from a volcano millions of years ago. There's this shear curtain of solid rock, leading down to a flat platform of rock that never gets overgrown. Must be something to do with the winds sweeping it clean."

"I'd like to see that."

"Yes, we should go down there. Today, how about we just open up the top end of one of the paths?"

They break out lopping and cutting tools, and set off around the back of the house. Sam points to the gully behind the house. "Wasn't that the place that was full of old fridges and stuff?"

"Yes. I cleared most of that away over the last few years. There's still junk in there, but mostly stuff that will rot away like old furniture, so I'm leaving it. We can check it out in a decade or two." He grins. "There, I must be getting used to this life, thinking long term again."

"Dad, we have a lot to learn about living the pre-industrial life. We have so little spare time, no Internet, no experts to call on except the people living right here."

There's a silence as they hack away at the undergrowth. The sun is high in the sky by the time they've cleared about 100m of path. "OK Sam, let's take a break. We need to hydrate, and collapse of civilisation or no, the ozone hole is still up there and we shouldn't stay out too much this time of day."

Back at the shack, they both take big drinks of rainwater.

"Dad, do you know what I really miss most?"

"Your mom?"

"Of course, and all our friends and family. But I mean what I miss of stuff."

His dad looks at him quizzically.

"Chocolate."

"Son, I wonder if we will ever see chocolate again. One of those bars has so much embedded in it. Cocoa beans from South America or Africa, vanilla, if it's the good kind, from somewhere like Madagascar. Then there's sugar, mostly grown in our coastal regions that are probably all wiped out for agriculture until the salinity washes through the topsoil."

For the first time, Sam looks tearful. "Dad, this is so silly. Millions dead in our own country, who knows how many around the world. Our family and friends gone, if we're lucky, somewhere we can't find them, if we're unlucky all dead. And here I am crying about chocolate."

Geoff pulls him close. "Son, you are not crying about chocolate. You are crying about everything that went away with it." Had he looked up, Sam would have seen his dad was crying too.

"OK boy, let's make some lunch then take a rest. We have work to do."

* * *

Time passes in increasingly meaningless units. Between doing more and more farm work in exchange for food, trying desperately to find ways to encourage their struggling veggie patch to grow and hacking out paths down to the valley, the shack is increasingly becoming a real home. There's even the odd item of furniture, donated by a farmer who appreciates good honest work, to fill out the cramped space.

Just once, they take the 4X4 towards the coast. Exactly as Geoff's assailant said, the road to the coast ends in a mess. There are trees strewn around like matchsticks, a boat beached somewhere in the distance, otherwise no evidence of human habitation. The Bruce Highway at this point is intact. Geoff looks up and down the highway. "It's amazing it got this far inland. Bruce Highway has to be cut off where it's closer to the coast." They head back in silence, Sam fiddling with the radio and picking up nothing.

After a few days of hard work, they decide they should take a weekend. They are sitting outside, admiring the bunyas.

"Dad, that was hard work on the farm yesterday, but I don't feel tired. Probably just as well we are walking so much now, not using the car much."

"Son, it's just as well our vehicle is a diesel and we didn't have to travel that far since refuelling. Even the odd five to ten Ks round trip will eventually not be an option by car."

"Well, you can run a diesel on veggie oil, right?"

"More or less. But like so many other things, I didn't
get around to finding out what modifications if any I need
to make to the engine, and we have no Internet now to ask.
In any case, where do we get that? No oil left in the shops.
And where would we go? After that trip where we saw there
really isn't much left past the Bruce highway, I'm not sure if
I want to find out more about what happened. So much for
my scientific curiosity.

"No use moping. How about we take a picnic down to
the basalt flow? We can celebrate my success at making
sourdough bread by taking sandwiches. And use up some of
that cheese that substituted for wages. If we start now, we
can be there by midday and take a break in the shade."

It's a coolish day but winter hasn't set in yet. As they pack
away the picnic lunch, Geoff says, "Let's pack something
warm in case it cools off before we get back."

Sam nods, and finds the rain jacket he wore that distant
day when they escaped Brisbane.

It's a bright sunny day with no cloud in the sky, a perfect
Queensland mountain autumn day. For once the walk down
the path isn't work. They aren't carrying tools or slashing
at invaders. The sun is near its zenith when they reach the
basalt. The rock is warm to the touch, even in a shaded spot
– warmth saved from when that patch was in full sun. They
stretch out on the warmed shaded patch, and pass around
chunks of bread and farm cheese. Geoff passes Sam a water

bottle.

Sam takes a long drag on the bottle. "Man, I could really use some chocolate now."

An hour or so passes, and the sun dips noticeably. "Dad, I suppose we should get back home. I can just imagine the magic of this place. All it will take is an army to chop out the lantana." The spiky creepers almost surround the rocky space.

Geoff smiles. "The world may be going to hell, but places like this still stir our inner humanity. Let's go. We can visit here whenever we like. Give or take our busy schedule."

The hike up the path is heavy going, but not hard work for their farm-hardened muscles. Near the top, they pause to look down. "Dad, does the path go near the top of the basalt flows? I can't tell with all the winding around the steep bits."

"Actually it does at a point, not too far down. There's a view site. I think I may be able to find it. We'll need to cut our way through. Sounds like work."

"Why not? If it's a spectacular view, I could do that on my day off."

They fetch machetes and loppers. It's almost dark when Geoff motions ahead. "I think that's about the place."

"Where, here?" Sam moves in the direction his dad is pointing and, with a cry, disappears. There's a series of crashes, then silence.

"Sam!" There's no answer. "Sam! It's getting dark. I'll try

to find you but if I can't, wrap up warm. It shouldn't get cold tonight."

Geoff rushes back to the shack to find a light. The torch batteries are low. He walks down the trail as far as he dares, shouting reassurance to Sam. Eventually he is forced to give up. *I'll never find him in the dark unless he can shout.* He has a sinking feeling about what that means. At first light, Geoff is on the trail with tools, rope and water. He shouts for Sam as he goes, and the only reply is distant bird calls. At the foot of the basalt flow he finds Sam, neck at an unnatural angle. Stone cold. Rigid. "My beautiful boy." Geoff holds him until he cannot deny it. His boy is dead.

Numbly he clears as much alien vegetation as he can around the horizontal basalt patch. He stacks it in the centre of the bare rock, and adds dry wood and twigs as tinder. He gently undresses the body, having to cut the clothes at times because of the rigor mortis. His son's slight frame is surprisingly hard to manoeuvre onto the pyre. He adds a pile of dead branches. Then Geoff sets a match to the driest twigs. After a few tries, they start to burn. He retreats to the side of the rock, tears from the smoke mixing with tears of loss. Slowly, the fire builds, until the heat is enough to catch the damp timber. The fire is burning with a roar. He can no longer see Sam's body. The flames reach several metres into the air, and the smoke forms a thick column.

Somewhere in the distance he is aware of car engines,

then voices. Too distant to make out, but he guesses they are at the shack. He doesn't care. If it's the yokels who assaulted him that first day, now here to rob him, or the kindly farmers who gave them work for food, it's all the same. He has nothing left.

Then the impossible sound – a slight throb then a steady beat. The chop-chop-chop of a helicopter. Then the copter is overhead, and someone descends on a rope. The figure on the rope looms larger, turns into someone in military fatigues. The chop-chop-chop recedes in the direction of the voices and stops.

Geoff looks up blankly at the stranger striding towards him.

"What's up mate? Are you in some kind of trouble? We saw your smoke signal clear from the other side of the mountain."

"It's not a smoke signal. Funeral pyre. My son died."

"I'm so sorry. Look, it's risky alone in a wild place like this. Let me walk you out."

"I know my way around pretty well. My back yard."

"I have to get out to the chopper. They aren't going to hover to pick me up now there isn't a rescue. Fuel's scarce, you know."

"I know."

"All right, let's go."

They start up the trail. Geoff is slowly coming to his

senses. "What are you doing here anyway? It's been months since the disaster, and you are the first outsider we've seen. I went hell for leather away from the coast after trying to warn people and, for all I know, my son and I are ... just me now I suppose ... all that's left of Brisbane."

"Tried to warn people?" His companion takes a close look at him for the first time. "I didn't recognize you with all that shaggy beard. Are you by any chance Dr Geoff Dawson?"

"I am. Why?"

"We are scouting for high-value survivors, people who can help get society back on its feet. A Liberal member happened to mention you as someone who irritatingly claimed we were all doomed, then the disaster struck. You were the only one who saw it coming."

"What good does that do?"

"Dr Dawson, you're a hero. We need you in Canberra to get things together again."

"And work with the Liberal member and other clowns in government who refused to listen, and laughed at me when they could have helped?"

"A flight into Sydney that night reported that the city had vanished, and everyone stopped laughing. We saved up to half the population. First wave took out the east coast power grid and everyone in lower areas. We managed to get people out before the second real monster wave. We don't know how many. Things are still a total mess. Canberra is a very different place. We have a government of national unity, with Greens in the cabinet. Believe me, they take you very seriously now."

"I'm sorry, this is all too much for me.   Let's keep walking."

"Of course. This has been a terrible time for us all, and this day particularly for you." The soldier reaches into his backpack. "We don't have a lot of this left, but you need it. Give you strength." He offers Geoff something in a colourful wrapper.

Geoff stares at the proffered bar in revulsion. Chocolate.

The Uncanny Valley

The signal is weak and Commander Firby grimaces with concentration. "Is he getting into a theological discussion? He's found the right person. The kingpin."

Lieutenant Jameson next to him is controlling the drone and raises an eyebrow in acknowledgement.

He thumbs the mike switch. "Andy, what are you waiting for?" He glances at Jameson whose thumbs down means that the view from the drone remains inconclusive. "Andy, we have nothing from the drone – we can't see into your physical location and there are too many people about. It has to be this way." Audio is fuzzy, but it sounds as if Andy is addressing the target as "imam" and asking existential questions.

Firby's finger hovers over the Execute control when the screen border flashes red. The image from the drone registers a satisfactory flash as the signal from Andy abruptly cuts off. Dust clears to show the tent blown apart and people on

72

the ground scattering.

Johannes Kepler Firby sighs. Another job well done. And Andy will have to be rebooted from backup.

He rises from his control chair, and stows his headphones as the drone circles conspicuously before it heads back to base. "Let them think it was the drone that bombed them. It worked before," he mutters to himself. Jameson ignores him, focused on removing his headphones. Time to debrief. He gathers up his mission documents and notes and stuffs them into a file stamped TOP SECRET, contemplating the irony of his old-fashioned preference for paper while working at the leading edge of military high tech. He nods to Jameson in the standby chair and they both head for the conference room, Jameson clutching a much thinner but equally secret folder.

The screens light up. General Wade appears on the centre screen. Firby starts briefly then realizes that the top brass had to be following this one, given the target. He throws a salute at the screen.

"At ease, soldier." Wade waits for the other screens to light up. One of them is the president. Another is Secretary of Defense Cartwright. Another screen lights up with a rear admiral whom Firby does not recognize.

"Are we all present? Mr President," Wade says, "Commander Firby is our chief droid controller on this mission. Commander?"

"Mr President." Firby pauses, unaccustomed to such a

high-powered meeting. "Mr President, our droid, Andy has with high certainty taken out Jihad Mohammed as the leader of the True Jihad faction styles himself. He made a positive ID and was in close proximity when he blew his charges."

"How positive is the identification?" The president leans towards the camera in anticipation.

"Close to 100%. Andy had on board biometrics – retina scans, DNA, facial recognition data, fingerprints. He was able to make a positive ID on face, retina and fingerprints. All of course unknown to the other side who saw him as just another recruit, keen to see the leader close up and personal."

"Well done, Commander. Sadly, we cannot go public with this and give you a citation though we will find a way to do so covertly."

"Of course the hard work was done by the intelligence team and Andy..."

"A machine," the general adds hastily.

Secretary of Defense Cartwright butts in: "Quite so, a machine. That it looks totally human and can fool people at short range at least under limited circumstances makes it effective. But we cannot allow the public the idea that we too are in the suicide bomber game. Just a machine."

The general nods. "Admiral, I believe your team is planning a review."

"That's right. The program has been immensely successful so far, but that does not mean it is without risk. Commander, we would like you to continue this debrief with the design team to ensure we minimize risk going forward. The Joint Chiefs will receive their report, hence General Wade's presence."

Firby squints uneasily at the rear admiral, with an uncomfortable feeling that he should know who this is. Why would he be reviewing the droid program? Is this a military audit office I don't know about? "So that would be why I am I facing this high-powered delegation rather than my usual post-mission debrief?"

"Commander, quite right. I would appreciate it if you do a low-key debrief of the mission itself while it is still fresh, and we will be convening the review as soon as we can get the key personnel together. It will not be a large panel, so get your debrief done ASAP. Your OC will be on the panel, so no need to include him in your mission debrief. You will report this last mission as part of your report on the overall program."

The president smiles. "Admiral Cohen, an ongoing run of successes is rare in military operations. We would like to keep it that way. Success, I mean – I did not intend making rare sound good." The president looks around. "Secretary, General Wade, anything to add?"

Firby finally places the rear admiral. Head of Navy Droids. Appointed about a month ago, but not yet able to free himself from Washington to visit the front line – here. He shakes his head. My head is too much in my work – I should know my own boss even if he's never bothered to visit me at work.

Secretary Cartwright smiles tightly as if not to upstage the president. "Not much from me. Just a caution. We must ensure that nothing leaks from this program. Nothing at all. Our competitive advantage in having this technology is huge and we cannot have it fall into the wrong hands. Nor for that matter can the public know that we are using something that looks like a human, in effect, as a bomb. The number of wrong messages that would send is incalculable."

The general adds: "Secretary, you and the president have made yourselves clear on a number of occasions. This is why we are conducting this review. We will have some civilian scientists on the review since they were involved in original research, but we will quarantine them from any discussion of combat applications – as far as they are concerned, we are purely using droids to replace humans in hazardous situations such as confronting active shooters or potential suicide bombers."

The Secretary turns to Firby. "Commander, your brief report please."

Recognizing an order not a request, Firby launches straight in.

"I need not go into details of Jihad Mohammed and his group. The main issue is they are extremely close-knit and selective in their recruiting. We had to use a real person in the early stages to be sure we didn't give away anything and were able to substitute Andy when he was passed between handlers. He functioned flawlessly; no one suspected he was anything but the original recruit. Once he was in position, we worked very hard to get a drone strike in place, but could not get sight of the target, nor could we be clear on proximity of civilian targets. So we had Andy move in close and he detonated himself when we made our final determination that there was no other option. We also had a drone conspicuously placed to give the appearance that it had caused the explosion."

The president looks troubled. "I don't like this 'he'. This is a machine. Even if some clown called the program Bourne Again. Which seems to have stuck, and we can't undo because the program does not officially exist. There is a huge difference between a human agent and a droid."

Firby nods. "I understand, Mr President. But we have to train them thoroughly in blending in seamlessly with humans and that means we talk to them ourselves as if they are humans. We cannot risk the uncanny valley."

To the president's quizzical look, Firby adds: "An idea going back to the 1970s. If we make robots seem more and more humanlike, people are more and more comfortable with them. But you hit a point where they look too lifelike – small glitches make them seem weird. That's the valley. On the other side of the valley, you have an android, a droid – a robot so humanlike, you can't see the difference."

"And this super-humanlike robot makes you uneasy if it suddenly breaks out of its role?"

"Yes, Mr President."

"Anyway, commander, remember it's just a machine." The President looks dismissive and that signals the end of the conference.

As the screens dim, Jameson talks for the first time. "Wow. That was some high-power telecon. I know we are doing pretty well, but Chairman of Joint Chiefs, Secretary, President and Head of Navy Droids all at once."

Firby looks grim. He shrugs off the disquiet that Jameson clearly knows who their boss is. "I just hope the slight hint of weirdness from Andy isn't a sign of trouble. Not now, not with eyes like this on us."

"Just Andy?"

"Nothing from any of the other droids yet. But he is the oldest, longest in the field, most reboots. He is the only one who's hesitated on carrying out an order as far as I know."

Jameson grins. "There is one thing that makes a politician even more uneasy than all this stuff."

"What's that?"

"Because of secrecy, the prez can't claim credit for Bourne Again, which he would dearly love to, given that he beat the person who started it."

They pick up their folders and walk out of the conference

room, reports on the last mission still stowed.

* * *

Heidelberg, Germany. Home of one of the world's oldest uni-
versities dating back to 1386, eleven Nobel Laureates to its
name. None a household name like Einstein (or even a fa-
mous non-winner like Stephen Hawking), but a respectable
achievement nonetheless. All of the awardees are in Physics,
Chemistry and Medicine. And that just counts professors at
Heidelberg. Other laureates include the illustrious Max Born,
who studied at Heidelberg; among those physicists, chemists
and medics, there is one Peace laureate, Albert Gobat, a PhD
graduate – again not a household name.

The Peace laureate aside, it seems Heidelberg has a rather
one-sided excellence in the physical and medical sciences. Yet
it is the medical field that has made it one of the leaders in android research, and which has placed it at the epicentre of the
top secret US Navy Bourne Again program.

Firby is sitting at a computer in the university library, reading through the university's illustrious history when Jameson
sidles in. They are both wearing civvies, the convention when
out of the base to avoid calling attention to the very military
project hiding around the corner from the university. Jameson takes a look at the Nobel laureates and winks.

"Trying to find your namesake?"

"Johannes Kepler was way before they had Nobels and

as an astronomer he wouldn't have fitted in with this bunch. Anyway my dad was an astronomy nut and I'm not. I was just paging through this stuff to get a sense of why Schultz would have made his big breakthroughs in android design here, so far ahead of what we have at home."

"Well, he would be pretty surprised to know what we are doing with his stuff if he was still around. Our tech people still talk to some of the scientists here of course since they are the world leaders. And we are also based here because it is a convenient cover for missions that need to be in close radio proximity to the Middle East. I think one of them might be dragged in for the civvie part of the review."

"Yeah, right. We've covered my reason for being here. What are you doing in the university library?"

"Looking for you. I know you like visiting here for peace and quiet. And you had your phone off, so you had to be somewhere that has to be phone-free."

Firby closes the web browser and glances around at the students surfing the web, some even doing work. "OK, let's go. Is it urgent, or can we grab a coffee on the way?"

"Not that urgent. A quick coffee we can get away with."

"And going the long way around?"

Jameson shakes his head wryly. Sightseeing doesn't quite fit 'not that urgently', it seems. Firby taps him on the shoulder. "Lighten up. I know we're doing serious work. It's just that I'm from a part of the world where 'old' is built before 1960 and I like the ambiance of this place."

As they walk out to the bus stop, Jameson asks, "That prof who just died, the founder of the project, how well did you know him, what was his name again?"

"Schultz? We met at meetings, not socially. Towards the end he was almost locked in the lab. Very intense, as if he was solving the world's problems. And maybe he was, in a way. I got to talk to him in detail only once or twice. I wish I could have talked more. He really knew his stuff. Not that the others are bad, but there was so much in his head that we can't ever know now. And I can't say I can specially remember any of the others as a standout expert."

The bus arrives.

* * *

Andy flicks his eyes around rapidly. They are sitting around a small table. To his left is a Lieutenant Commander with longish blonde hair and a face that conveys disdain for conventions of femininity. On the right, Lieutenant Jameson. Facing Andy is Firby.

Firby breaks the ice. "Welcome back, Andy. You know my backup and drone controller Jameson, but I don't recall introducing Lieutenant Commander Fritzon. She is also a droid controller, usually works with Denny."

"Ah, yes. I have heard of her." Andy has a youthful voice to match his late-teen looks. He is darkly tanned, with colouring that could be Hispanic or Middle Eastern. "Denny and I compare notes."

"I'm sure you do. Anyway, we are here for a debrief of the last mission, but there is a bit more than that. The entire program is to be reviewed, and we want to be sure there are no surprises. When I thought I was having a mission debrief, instead of the usual meeting of fellow controllers and my immediate superiors, we had the president, no less, and chairman of Joint Chiefs, and others not much below those levels. So this is an informal debrief, under the shadow of a review."

Fritzon frowns. "Chair *man*, huh. Can they not even allow the chance that a woman could do the job?"

Jameson grins but Firby stays serious. "Now, Janet, in our circles we know there is no one better than you. It's just a matter of time..."

"Never mind that. Are we in trouble or is this routine?" Janet Fritzon is back to business.

"Good question, Janet. That's why we have Andy here. I think on the whole the project is going amazingly well. We are not only hitting all our targets with no casualties but we are sowing confusion on the other side. Each jihadist group thinks another is sending suicide bombers into their midst, betraying them to drones or both. Fighting between them has increased and some of the confusion we've sown has turned real. They actually are trying to destroy each other to an increasing extent.

"No." Firby turns to Andy. "The operational side is on the whole fine, but we need to talk to Andy about how he is holding up."

Andy looks at him coolly. "No casualties. You know, it is *very disconcerting* being blown up. You are in one place, then you are somewhere else. Your memories, depending on bandwidth up to the time of explosion, become patchy, like a badly-made video with poor audio.

"You guys gave us a sense of humour so we could pass for human. But Bourne Again? That's sick – but having read the original book, I can identify."

Jameson shakes his head. "Bourne Again is not my idea of a good name. But look: you were made for this. Of course you are blown up – that's if we can't use your intel to send in a drone and you find an exit. You save lives. If we sent in a drone every time, many more people would be killed. And you don't die. Here you are in your base body as if nothing had happened. We make you a new mission body, put this one to sleep, feed it memories with the highest bandwidth we can from the mission body until it destructs, then here you are, back again. And when your body gets decrepit, we give you a new one. Seems OK to me. When I wear out, I slow down and eventually die."

"Of course I have some advantages. I am just saying, it's *disconcerting*. I sometimes wish I could retire from combat, same way as humans."

"Your problem is you're too valuable," says Firby. "Every time you go out, you add to that store of experience. Sure, some of it is low bandwidth, but we can move it between droid minds a lot more efficiently than between anything else and humans. We are talking now, which is what you have to do with humans, but you can update your alternate body at the level of pure data.

"Anyway, that brings me to what I really wanted to ask. Last mission, just before execution, you seemed to be in a theological discussion with the target. What was that about?"

"That? Let me try to work it out from my patchy memory." Andy pauses for all of a second, his eyes briefly unfocused. "Right, it was something the imam in London told me, when I was establishing credentials by talking radical to outsiders, that the radical jihadists' idea of afterlife was flawed and that because their understanding of Islam was wrong, they would not get the afterlife they expected. I was curious as to whether this other imam had a different perception of afterlife."

"Did he?" Jameson chips in.

Andy turns to face him. "No. I don't think so. Just maybe a different set of conditions for access. Sorry, the detail is fuzzy. The link was not great."

Fritzon looks intrigued. "So why are you interested in

afterlife at all?"

"It seems to me an interesting reward and punishment system. If no one knows for sure what the rules are for entry, how do they justify conducting warfare on that basis? I have never asked any of my controllers this. Do you all have a way into this afterlife?"

Firby grins. "I am a Catholic. We have very specific views on this and those are rather different than the Islamic conception of how to go to Heaven and what sends you to Hell. We even have a refinement called Purgatory, where you go if you are not bad enough for Hell but need some help getting to Heaven." He looks intently at Andy.

Andy looks serious. "Do I get an afterlife?"

Firby shakes his head. "Why do you need an afterlife? You have a backup. Anyway in most belief systems, afterlife is specific to humans."

"I wouldn't be so sure. A lot of people believe in pet heaven and there is that whole eastern reincarnation thing," adds Fritzon unhelpfully.

"Janet, I'm not sure we want to confuse things more than we need to. Andy," Firby puts a hand on his shoulder, "don't worry yourself too much about this. We make you look as much like a human as we can, but you are something else, a different part of creation, so the same rules don't have to apply."

* * *

The conference room is dark as they file in. Then the sensors flick on the lights. The screens remain dim. This time, everyone talking is physically present.

The military men walk in first, followed by a civilian, and sit around the table.

The admiral tidily places his briefcase on the table and does the introductions. "This exploratory meeting is about getting to know everyone. I take it you all know who I am since I am your OC. For the record, I am Rear Admiral Felix Cohen, officer commanding, Android Division, though more officially, Special Projects, since androids do not officially exist."

A few grins and knowing nods around the room while he points as he speaks. "Commander Firby, senior handler. Lieutentant Jameson, backup handler. Lieutenant Commander Fritzon, senior backup handler.

"I think you all know Professor Schoon by reputation. Professor, could you introduce yourself?"

The professor looks like the stereotype of an academic, slightly shabby, stooped gait, out of touch with his surroundings. His movements are quick, even sharp, but not totally co-ordinated. He reveals all this just nodding and looking around the room. "Ja, thank you rear admiral." He pronounces the two words of the honorific separately with comical effect and Firby resists the temptation to correct him – the conventional form of address is "Admiral".

Schoon goes on after a pause, as if collecting his thoughts. "I work very much in the shadow of the late Professor Schultz, I think known to some of you. It was his brilliance that made the connection between advanced prostheses and artificial organs, leading to androids. We very much miss his insights and detailed knowledge but sadly, for all his excellence as a researcher, he was not able to save himself. The cancer was too aggressive."

Another pause.

"I am sorry, I digress. What you want to know is what I do, not a history lesson. I was a postdoctoral researcher under the good professor. I had just finished my doctorate when Bosnia fell apart and he was so good as to take me in. I put that past behind me and took on a German name. For these reasons I am totally dedicated to the professor's legacy and am delighted that his creations are being used to save lives. I wish though there was less secrecy. I personally would be very pleased if his name could appear on a headline when one of our androids stops a suicide bomber or does some other good deed.

"I am sorry, I dwell on the past again. So my role in the project is working on making androids as lifelike as possible, functioning as closely as possible to humans. My team is very proud of the way they can not only refuel themselves by consuming food as humans do, but that they can do it in a way that no one would suspect they were not human."

Firby is wondering where this is all leading – they all knew the German team's role in the underlying research – so he puts up his hand and asks, "Professor, thanks – I think we all know that. What would interest me is to understand what in our current designs would show an android up as *not* human. There may be scenarios where one has to be in the field a while, or even has to get through a medical. The brain structure, for example, from what little I understand, is not at all based on a human brain."

"Ja, at a detailed level, it works very differently. Our android brain is at heart a quantum computer. If you do a brain scan or even elementary chemistry analysis, it will look very human. If, however, you look at the electrical signals, subtly not so. The right parts fire up but not exactly as you would expect. At detail level of course very different."

Firby frowns and says quizzically, "Uncanny valley."

"Ja, exactly. It will look wrong, but you will not be sure why. You cannot put the finger on it."

"Right," says the admiral briskly. "We know all about that place. Professor, I think the Commander has asked a very relevant question. I don't think we need worry about brain scans. What concerns us more is getting through basic medicals – if one of our droids breaks a leg when it's in a place outside our control, for example, will we get away with that? Can they survive extended social interactions? We need to know if we can deploy them for extended periods where we suspect a risk."

Jameson butts in for the first time. "Real basic things like taking a leak. If your droid is playing the role of an Islamic militant for example . . . " Firby gives him a look, flicking his eyes to the professor, who is not cleared for top secret. Jameson goes on: " . . . say we have a militant cell we suspect of setting up suicide bombing and want to get in close to prevent it happening,"

"Ja, ja. I see what you mean. Our androids can pretty much get away with anything short of sex and we are working on that."

Fritzon speaks up for the first time. "Why *do* we make all the droids male? Surely the female anatomy is not that hard to the extent that we have to fake it?"

Professor Schoon creases his brow. "I am very much afraid that our focus has been to get one thing right first and since the brief from the military was to mimic a human in an emergency setting, we didn't think anyone would notice that this small number of, so to speak, heroic people were all male."

The admiral intervenes. "Look, people, Fritzon does have a point, that we may well need to create a perception of female action heroes who die for a good cause or indeed that there are cases where a 'female' droid will be necessary. But before we get there, we must review what we have. Professor, is there anything else about droids that could alert the public, a step into the uncanny valley, if you will."

"Ja, well there are one or two things. For one thing, they have another sense. To them, data is another sense. They are permanently wired into a network, one that they sense directly in the same way as they hear or see. This could give them away in ways we have not thought of. Another one is they have backups, so they are less likely to fear death than humans."

Jameson is about to talk but Firby preempts him – fearing another foray into terrain dangerously close to secrets to be kept from the civilian. "Professor, that is very interesting. Recently I was talking to one of our droids who had survived destruction by reverting to a backup and he didn't seem happy about that."

Schoon nods slowly. "Ja, I can imagine that could be *very*, ah, *disconcerting*. In one place then suddenly – *poof* you are somewhere else."

Jameson now manages to get his point in. "Data as a sense. Could you expand on that? Does that give them some sort of hive mind capability?"

"You mean a collective intelligence? No, that can't work. The delays over the network are too big. More perhaps like a shared experience, when they are permitted to connect and of course we control that, as you know. I think it is really more like vision except from a more diverse data source."

Fritzon grins. "Maybe we humans should try something

like that. We would not have to fight racism, gender discrim-
ination and so on if we saw the world from each other's point
of view."

The admiral is looking impatient. "I don't have all day
to discuss philosophy. Let's end this now and I suggest the
operational team draws up a comprehensive list of questions
for the professor. This meeting was about getting to know
each other, and that as far as I am concerned has gone as well
as could be expected." He gathers up his unopened briefcase
and gestures to the professor, who follows him out.

Firby stares at his fellow handlers, who all have a look
of someone who's woken up in an uncanny valley. "*Very
disconcerting.* Now where have I heard that before?"

$$* * *$$

He feels warm. He opens his eyes, turns away from the harsh
brightness, blinks. Then there is a shadow over his face. He
turns to face the shadow and feels coolness on his back as it
touches the bench – the bench he is lying on. His garment
has a gap at the back.

He looks up to the source of the shadow. It is large, a not
unfriendly dark face atop a strongly-built body. The body is
clad in dark blue and is topped with a cap. There is a badge
somewhere too; it is all too much and he blinks again.

The mouth opens and words form. "Aren't you supposed
to be in hospital?"

He sits up and the words register. "Hospital? Isn't that were sick people go?" He is confused. He feels well. Physically. He shakes his head. Mentally, he feels fine too. But he is confused and nothing makes sense.

A policeman. A memory. The policeman nods. "I don't know what is wrong with you but people only wear a gown like that in a hospital. Do you remember anything?"

He hesitates, then says haltingly: "No. No, ... I just woke up on this bench. I don't know how I got here."

"What is your name? Where do you live?"

He suddenly feels a rush of panic and sits up abruptly. "I have no idea." The action of sitting is strangely reassuring. Physical competence. Words are coming to him. He knows how to describe where he is. A park. Close to a beach. Nothing about it is familiar but he recognizes things. A bike path. A footpath. Cyclists. Pedestrians. In the distance, waves. Further, ships.

The policeman shows decision. "You showed no weakness sitting up. Can you walk?"

He stands up and takes a step. The hospital gown flaps loose behind him and he reflexively closes it.

The policeman nods. "Come with me to the station. My car is right here. We can try to work out who you are and what to do about you."

The car has a blue light on the roof and stripes on the side. The central stripe is blue, surrounded by yellow stripes.

The word "Police" is prominently emblazoned, along with a badge. It invokes thoughts of police but the detail feels wrong. He notes other writing: "Crime Stop" and a number. It is all so unfamiliar. He feels he should know what a police car looks like. He walks to the right-side front door. The cop motions to the other side; he has approached the steering wheel.

After a short ride through unfamiliar streets, they arrive at a large brick building with a secured entrance. He cannot shake the feeling of being in in the wrong place. Concepts like police, driving cars, street scenes and so on keep seeming familiar yet wrong, as if he is on the wrong side of a mirror.

Inside the police station, the cop takes him to a bare room with a table and chairs. "Wait here. I will fetch a superior to help." The cop removes his cap revealing crinkly hair: distinctly African. Another recollection. From where?

The cop returns promptly with another, much skinnier cop, in a jacket and tie, a firearm strapped to his waist. The newcomer has a businesslike look to him. He is a little lighter-skinned than the first cop and has straighter hair. "Constable Nxele" – the name has an unfamiliar click sound – "says he found you asleep on a bench near the waterfront. Can you tell us which hospital you were in?" Something in his head aligns. This man must be a detective. Not uniformed.

"No. I don't recall being in hospital."

"Never?" asks the detective.

"I can't say never. I don't remember anything before I woke up."

"And you don't remember how you got to Port Elizabeth?"

His brow creases. "I don't even know where Port Elizabeth is. Everything here seems strange. I recognize things like palm trees along the roads. But the roads seem wrong somehow, everything is back to front."

The constable looks at him knowingly. "You tried to get into the car on the wrong side. You have an American accent. So you would be used to driving on the other side. If you forgot where you were ..."

The detective gives the constable a look as if to say this is my gig. "So you are probably an American citizen then? We will contact your consulate and see if they have any idea who you are. In the meantime we will check hospitals. As a foreigner you must have been at a private hospital. Do you really not remember a thing?"

He shakes his head. "I really remember nothing – things come to me like what a car is, what police are and so on – but the detail is all wrong."

The constable says: "As if you woke up in the wrong place?"

As he responds with "Yes, that is so *disconcerting*," he goes cold. This is something he has heard before. He shakes his head but fails to clear it.

"Constable, can you start by phoning all the local hospitals? Check government ones as well to be on the safe side. If anyone is missing a patient, that should help. Particularly one with memory loss. I will phone the American consulate in Cape Town."

"Right, sir. Meantime, though, can I get our guest some tea?"

The detective is about to retort but decides better of it. "OK, if you can organize something, that is up to you. But I want to hear from those hospitals."

An hour later, the constable reappears and notes the empty teacup. "I have asked all the hospitals and the American consulate knows of no one of your description has who been reported as missing. My superior says I should take you to Elizabeth Donkin for psychiatric evaluation."

"Elizabeth Donkin?"

"A government hospital. We can get a government psychiatrist to try to work out what the memory loss problem is about."

"And did you ask them if they knew about someone like me?"

"I did. I said *all* of the hospitals. No one is missing a patient."

* * *

Elizabeth Donkin is not a large hospital. He knows this without a recollection of what any other hospital looks like.

The constable leads him to a doctor – a psychiatrist. She seems friendly. She is sitting at a desk with a computer and is facing him. He is in a marginally comfortable chair. The room is bare, undecorated.

Constable Nxele stands at his side. "Excuse me doctor. I should introduce your patient but he doesn't have a name. I have been thinking of him in my head as X."

He swivels in the chair and asks "X? Is that rather generic as an unknown?"

Nxele smiles. "Try pronouncing my name. It is spelled N-X-E-L-E. The 'X' is a click sound in our language that foreigners struggle with so many of my friends with names starting with an X in self-defence call themselves 'X'. So calling you X is not so foreign to me."

X nods appreciatively, "Thanks, but what do I call you then? Not also X?"

"No, no. If you want to be formal, Constable. But my first name is Ben. That is also a defence: my Xhosa name is too hard for foreigners." The word 'Xhosa' starts with a click too.

"Koa-sa," says X uncomfortably and quizzically.

"Our language."

The doctor takes charge. "Thank you Constable. You can leave me with the patient. We can work on his isXhosa pronunciation later." Despite her Caucasian appearance, she says the click convincingly, at least to X's ears.

Nxele nods and walks out. She waits for the door to close.

"I am Dr Coetze." She notes his puzzled expression. "The constable said you had this feeling of waking up in the wrong place. Does my name trigger anything?"

"The opposite. It is part of the strangeness, not a name I have encountered before. At least I think I can pronounce it, unlike the constable's." He tries and judging from her expression, manages to mangle it.

She makes some notes. Her hair is greying and she has a slight build – a mouse – that's what she reminds him of. A tame unthreatening mouse. Threatening? He feels anxiety. What could be a threat? The feeling passes as she speaks again.

"It seems we are doing well triggering a feeling of strangeness. Perhaps we should try to find something familiar that may unlock a memory or two. I am not a great expert on American accents, but I don't think yours is from the South. Does that ring any bells?"

He shakes his head slowly. "Texas."

"You have a memory of Texas?"

"No. I just remembered it is in the South."

"That's something. Let's keep going with place names." She looks down at her computer and starts reading slowly, watching for a reaction. "Boston. New York. Michigan. Minneapolis. Chicago. Denver. California. Colorado."

She pauses. "I thought I saw a reaction when I mentioned California."

He concentrates. "Yes, maybe. Can you try a few places in California?"

"So you remember it's a state?" As he confirms she pays attention to the screen. "I don't use Google Maps a lot but let me try. Sacramento. San Francisco. San José." She pronounces the last as *Josie* and he stops her.

"That's San José. Spanish J is like an English H."

"So you have a memory of San José?" This time, she mangles it into *San Hosie*.

His face is a picture of introspection. "No, not really. I just remember how to pronounce it."

She looks frustrated then composes herself. "Memory loss is a peculiar thing, particularly if there is no physical cause. You seem otherwise healthy, though I will order some tests. Sometimes it just comes back like that –" she clicks her fingers – "or it can be a slow and tedious process.

"On thing for sure: I cannot put you out in the street like this. Since no one has claimed you, we can admit you as a state patient so you will have a place to stay. Ordinarily we would have to admit you to a general hospital first for observation but I can pull a few strings. That would be pointless in your case."

"Do I have any choice?"

"Not really – we can't discharge you with no idea what your underlying condition is. I will however ask the police to try a bit harder to track your origins down. If we can get a

DNA swab and fingerprints, your government may be able to find something."

"Fine – tell me what to do."

"We will get the police forensics unit in to take care of the details. In the meantime, I will send for an orderly to take you to admissions. I'm afraid as a state hospital we will not be offering you the luxury you may be accustomed to."

"I wish I knew what that was."

"Let me put it this way. At least you are physically strong so you should survive."

On that promising note she reaches for the phone and speaks for some time showing growing evidence of frustration and eventually crashes the receiver down. "It will be on the whole easier if I walk you to admissions. Follow me.

"The administrative staff can be obstructive. They are demanding details like an ID or passport number. You don't even have a name. A psychiatric hospital can admit people without ID – it is the nature of the place."

After much wrangling, X is in a ward with patients in various states of hopelessness. He instinctively straightens up his bed and tidies the blanket. *Mil spec* pops into his mind but he keeps it to himself.

Dr Coetze says: "I will leave you until tomorrow; a little rest may clear your head. Then we can work on a treatment programme."

He sits on the bed, watching her briskly departing form.

His next thought is that if you were not admitted for depression, this place would fix that. He looks around the ward and the other patients show no interest. He walks over to the window and looks out. It is a sunny day but windy. Nothing he sees triggers a memory. He sits on the bed and closes his eyes for an indeterminate time. Something is going on – a quiet background murmur he has not paid attention to before. It has no direction, no structure.

After making no progress in trying to make sense of this, he opens his eyes and sees the familiar form of Constable Nxele, who has brought someone else with him, who is carrying a briefcase. The newcomer is of much slighter build than Nxele but has similar features – at least to the unpracticed non-African eye. He is not in uniform and wears the non-stylish plain clothes that gives him away as a cop.

Nxele's face brightens up. "Ah, I see you recognize me. So you are not forgetting things that happened today. I brought Sergeant Mene from forensics. He is going to take your fingerprints and a DNA swab so the Americans can try to match you to their database. Then we will know if you are somebody." Nxele laughs. "Of course you are somebody. Excuse my English."

"No apology needed. What must I do?"

Mene says: "If you can open your mouth I can take a swab for DNA." That out of the way, Mene produces a fingerprint kit and efficiently takes a set of prints.

X watches as Mene packs away his kit. "Constable, will I see you again soon?"

Nxele smiles. "Of course. I will be back tomorrow. It is such a nice change to investigate someone who's pleased to see me."

* * *

A bright shiny morning in a dull place. X sits up in bed. He has been issued with hospital pyjamas, a step up from a hospital gown open at the back. It imparts some dignity. He rubs his chest and runs his right hand over his left arm. Everything feels very real, very solid.

He feels in need of exercise, movement. Anything but being confined to this grey lifeless space. The other patients all have a look of being on drugs – none stirs despite the growing early-morning sunlight. He judges it to be summer based on the quality of light, and hence early.

He steps out of bed and feels the urge to do push-ups. He is at fifty when he senses a presence and stops. It is Nxele again, with a stranger. "Apologies; I did not expect visitors. My head may be questionable but at least my body is not and I needed to test that."

X gets up onto the bed and does a double take. The newcomer looks startlingly like himself – different in detail but similar features. He has not looked at himself in a mirror yet he senses the resemblance – and the difference. Again:

the non-specific feeling that something is not quite right.

Nxele says: "No need for apology. It is after all rather early. But I thought you would be happy to know we have a positive result from your government. They know who you are. Your name is David Cramer, and we have a visitor from your consulate. I met him on my way into the hospital."

The stranger introduces himself. "Good morning. I am Fredrick Jones, and we are very pleased you have turned up. I have a new passport for you and will be escorting you to the airport. We have a flight booked at 8am, which will connect to a flight out of the country in Johannesburg. We will have you home and with your family without delay."

He hands over a passport. "I will be accompanying you. I also have some cash you can use for expenses on the way." He hands over a wad of currency – some X does not recognize but assumes is local; the rest is $100 bills.

X takes the money without interest and puts it under his pillow. He pages through the passport carefully, noting the photo page with the name. Perhaps it looks like him – but it could also be his visitor.

The visitor is looking at him expectantly. X slowly comes to a conclusion. "I am not ready to go. I have profound memory loss and I need to get a diagnosis."

Jones remonstrates: "But your family, the US government –"

X stares at him coldly. "Yes, the US government. You say

you are from the consulate. Do you have any ID? A passport? Proof of credentials?"

"I have *your* passport. I left my own passport in my car, as it happens. But why do I have to prove my credentials? Who else could deliver you a passport?"

"I don't care. Go away. I need time. And when you come back, bring convincing proof of who you are."

Jones prepares to argue and Nxele intervenes. "Look, he has a point. He isn't under arrest. We have no allegation of an offence or that he is in the country legally. You cannot force him to leave. However, I can force you to leave. This hospital is in my country, not yours."

Jones looks angry but backs off. Nxele sees him out of the ward then watches through the window until he drives off.

X is staring at him. "Thank you. I didn't expect you to support me like that."

"I know the type – expect to get their way. If he forced you to go with him, it would be abduction. If you are on the run from the US, they should extradite you. If you are an illegal immigrant, my government will send you on your way. Until any of that happens, no one can force you to do anything.

"But tell me now: why were you so suspicious? Oh, and by the way, nice move keeping the money."

"He did give it to me unconditionally and made no move to take it back."

X counts the money. Local notes say *200* in large print

and in fine print *TWO HUNDRED RAND.* "How much does twenty thousand rand buy?"

"It is more than I make in a month but my job doesn't pay so well. You have a pile of dollars too."

"I *think* I know what those buy. Can I spend them here?"

"Not legally. You need to go to a foreign exchange dealer and you need a passport."

"I have a passport now. That's what made me suspicious. How does a passport to appear so fast? Where did they find a photo of me? You normally use a new one each time. Jones looks enough like me that it could be his passport."

"If his name is Jones. Tell you what. I'll check with the consulate whether they sent someone called Jones to pick you up. If not, I will arrest him as soon as he shows up again."

"Thanks. In the meantime, could you take me to buy me clothes? I imagine the hospital won't stop me going. They only checked me in because I had no place to go."

"How many push ups did you do when we walked in?"

"About 50. Why?"

"Definitely nothing wrong physically. And after the way you dealt with that crook, your head can't be that bad. Let's talk to the doctor but I am sure it will not be a problem."

It wasn't and they soon are at a shop called Woolworths. X looks around in bewilderment. Nxele wrinkles his brow. "Another wrong thing?"

"The name is familiar. But not quite right ... Looks way

too classy. And ... I just remembered. *Woolworth*: went bust more than 20 years ago."

A few people are giving them odd looks because of X's hospital pyjamas but the Nxele's police uniform seems to settle them and they look away.

"This is the place the larneys get clothes. Too expensive for me but you have enough cash."

"Larneys" is new on X as well but he lets it pass and picks out a pack of boxer shorts, some robust-looking jeans, short-sleeved cotton shirts, socks and sturdy-looking shoes.

"Aren't you going to try them on?"

"Just the shoes. I have an eye for size."

"Did you just remember that?"

"You're right, I did."

After paying, X ducks into the toilet to change into his new clothes, bagging the extras along with the pyjamas in large stylish carry bag the store provided. "OK, I guess you are in a hurry to get back to the station, otherwise someone will be asking after you."

"Right. Let's go."

In the police car, Nxele has obviously taken note of the time he's been away and floors it. X stays calm – Nxele appears to know what he's doing though he is clearly in violation of all manner of traffic laws.

At the station, Nxele leads the way to his desk. "OK, let me try to get the American consulate in Cape Town."

After various calls he eventually gets the consulate. "Hello. Do you have someone there called Jones who was sent to Gqeberha – Port Elizabeth – this morning? Frederick Jones? ...no ..."

X grabs the receiver. "Hi, can you tell me anything about David Cramer?"

The voice on the other end sounds puzzled. "Mr Cramer? He has taken a few days off. A personal matter ..."

"Thank you. Thank you very much."

As X hands the phone back to Nxele he nods grimly; X says: "Exactly as I guessed. Cramer had a passport ready for me because it was his own. It happened that I look close enough to him that he could get away with that. How he organized an unused one, issued today, at such short notice is interesting."

"So what do we do now?"

"I don't think it is safe for me at the hospital."

Before Nxele can respond, another cop appears in the doorway and addresses Nxele. "There's someone in the charge office demanding to see you. He says you are creating an international incident and will take it higher if you do not sort it out at once."

Nxele follows his colleague at a rapid clip, followed by X.

Jones is there, looking agitated. "You are detaining an American citizen without charge."

"No he's not," says X. "I am here voluntarily. You still

have not established who you are."

"Well, here is my passport. A US diplomatic passport. It shows my name and photo. You cannot get more official than that."

"Now here's the thing. We called the consulate in Cape Town and they know of no Frederick Jones. But an employee called David Cramer has taken a few days off. This passport is completely unused and looks new. I think it's a fake and you're trying to abduct me. Constable, is that sufficient grounds to arrest him?"

Nxele shakes his head. "This is above my level. I'm still in uniformed. You cannot get a more junior policeman. I'll call the station commander." He turns to one of the other cops and whispers in his ear. He scurries off and returns shortly with a strongly-built caucasian female with short blonde hair.

She looks at X, then Jones, then Nxele. "Righto, what's going on?"

Jones opens his mouth but Nxele beats him to it. "Colonel, this man showed up at the waterfront yesterday morning in a hospital gown and with no memory. I took him to Elizabeth Donkin and they found nothing wrong with him except his memory. Our enquiries to the Americans because of his accent led to *this* man" – he points to Jones – "showing up at the hospital claiming to be from their consulate in Cape Town. I just phoned the consulate and they've never heard of Frederick Jones, which is what he calls himself. He produced a passport back at the hospital for our visitor in the name David Cramer. But a David Cramer working at the consulate has taken a few days off.

"So this looks very suspicious. Our visitor, who we are calling X, is accusing this man of trying to abduct him."

X adds: "If he has this alleged diplomatic passport and his consulate doesn't know him, that is really suspicious. I insist that he be held for attempted abduction."

The colonel looks troubled. Diplomatic immunity is not something to take lightly. "I cannot arrest him unless I am sure that there is a problem with his passport. Mr Jones, could you accompany me to my office while I make some calls? Constable, stay here." She picks up Jones's passport.

Jones is clearly not happy. "No, ma'am. I will not accompany you anywhere. Are you unfamiliar with the basics of diplomatic immunity?"

"Of course I am. But if there's evidence that the passport is a forgery, I ... "

"Have you any idea what kind of trouble you will be in if you pursue this?"

The colonel puts the passport down. She turns to Jones and says icily, "I also have some idea what kind of trouble there will be if I don't and it turns out there are solid grounds for suspicion."

A raging argument ensues and while they are distracted, X pockets the Jones diplomatic passport. In a brief break in the shouting, he says, "Apologies for interrupting. This is obviously going to take time to sort out. Could the constable take me to a coffee shop while you work it out? I missed breakfast."

The station commander obviously does not entertain being interrupted and is about to give X a piece of her mind when he holds up a hand to stop her. "I am hungry and confused. I mean no disrespect."

She grunts and refocuses on Jones. Nxele leads X away before anyone can stop them. As they head out of the station, Nxele says, "Neat move, palming that passport."

"Oh. You saw that."

Nxele laughs. "It goes with my job. I have seen plenty of crooks in my time. But you aren't one: he is as bent as a jailed politician. Without his diplomatic passport he's nothing. I would love to know how he sorts it out but I am delegated to take you for breakfast."

Over cappuccino and eggs, X takes his bearings. "I really am not ill. Except for this memory thing. Whatever Jones is up to, I would rather he did not find me again. Perhaps a hotel? But if he has the resources to rustle up a diplomatic passport in a few hours, he could track me down there too."

Nxele looks thoughtful. "The police cells are pretty safe. But even less luxurious than the hospital. You are not accused of a crime; I could I suppose arrest you on suspicion of being an illegal immigrant but that seems unfair when we know nothing about you. And then I can't just let you out of jail once you are arrested without a lot of explaining. Tell you what: how about you sleep tonight at my home? Then I can keep an eye on you."

"Won't you get in trouble?"

"I don't see why. You aren't under arrest. I agree that hospital isn't safe with strange people trying to abduct you. I will talk to my superiors to make sure there is no problem. It may be a bit irregular but this is easier for them than putting a police guard at the hospital."

Back at the station, Nxele checks at the charge office. No one knows where the Colonel or the fake diplomat has gone. Nxele says: "I have a lot of paperwork to catch up. How about you just sit with me while I do that? If no one appears to tell me what to do by the time I knock off, we can just go home together."

"Fine."

X closes his eyes and feels a susurration of background noise that has almost faded and is moving to the fore again, that is strangely familiar. Indeterminate time passes. Suddenly he senses snatches of conversation.

How did he get away?

There are no sounds, but he senses different personalities.

There's a limit to how fast we can make passports.

There is other noise, not part of the conversation. But the

critical bits are clear.

Who would have thought the South African Police would be so difficult? Normally a junior cop is ...

Detail is lost in the noise.

How did we lose that diplomatic passport? Not easy to make on short notice.

Best guess. He took it. So he has two identities but we know them both.

Yes, but one is diplomatic. If he has any idea, he can use it to slip under the radar.

Then the noise is too extreme to pick out anything intelligible. He opens his eyes. Nxele is talking anxiously on his cell. X catches his eye. Nxele finishes the call. "Robbery in town. Lots of the messaging. But I don't think I will be involved. Not my sector and it's not big enough to call in all sectors."

Nxele turns to look at X. "You look as if you woke up and saw a ghost."

"Almost. I told you I was in good health except for memory so don't take this the wrong way. I am picking up conversations between people who are after me."

Nxele looks concerned. "Voices in your head?"

"No. Not really – it is as if I was tapping their phone calls. I couldn't actually *hear* voices. Very weird. I picked up that they tricked up the diplomatic passport at short notice and were worried that I could use it. Then there was too much noise to make sense of anything else – about when you started using your phone."

"Maybe I do need to take you to that doctor again. But look – it's been a long day. I am on early shift so I can go home now. I am still happy to take you with me as I promised.

"The passport story is interesting. It seems they tried a quick and dirty thing of giving you a passport that already existed then when that failed, faked a new one for themselves to try to use diplomatic immunity. Tomorrow, we can worry about who can do that sort of thing in a matter of hours. They will not follow us into the township. They would be too conspicuous there."

Nxele's home is quite a trip out of the city. They take a taxi – a crammed minibus. Big yards and well-built houses fade into scenes of trash and small run-down houses. After their stop, they walk for about 10 minutes. Nxele's house is small with a rough fence but the interior is clean and inviting. Interior walls are bright, strong colours and windows have friendly curtains concealing serious burglar bars. Modest furnishings look well-used but not decrepit. "Welcome to my castle."

X almost breaks down. "You have no idea what it feels like to be in a friendly place. I only have memories since yesterday and I have no idea what it feels like to have a home, except the feeling that I *should* know. That hospital was so depressing."

"Well good. If you remember nothing, you will not find my humble dwelling too modest. My wife gets home later.

She teaches at a school nearby. I am sure she will cook us something nice."

"Cook? I know how to cook a few things."

"Like what?"

"I don't know."

"Ah, the memory. Stop worrying. Sit down and let's have a beer."

Nxele returns with two large bottles. Seeing X's expression, he says: "Beer strange to you to?"

"I know what beer is. But the bottle is unfamiliar. I don't know the brand and the size looks wrong."

Nxele opens both bottles. "Only one thing to do: taste. Then tell me if it's strange."

X samples his. "I am sure I had a beer something like this before. I think. My memory of taste is hazy. Beer. Coffee. Eggs. These are such distinctive things, flavours you cannot mistake – yet it is as if I know of them. As if someone told me what they were but I had never tasted anything before."

"X, you are a puzzle. But not one to solve now. Sit back, relax."

They settle down to watch television: local news. X absorbs what he can, not making much sense of anything. In the meantime dull noises in his head persist, but nothing as clear as the earlier conversation.

The door opens and Nxele's wife breezes in. Nxele jumps up and makes the introductions. "X, meet Gladys."

She examines X quizzically. "You don't look like an X."

Nxele laughs. "I told him about that nickname. His is the western version: X for unknown. I found him on the beachfront yesterday and he has no memory of his past. We thought he was American. Someone claiming to be from the Cape Town American consulate tried to take him away this morning but the whole thing was very fishy. He doesn't have a place to stay so I brought him home."

"You would bring a guest when I have nothing to cook. I hope your guest likes umngqusho."

X looks at Nxele for guidance. "Samp and beans. Samp is dried mealies and beans are beans."

"Mealies?"

"Ah, corn. Another thing wrong?"

Gladys looks ascance. "Wrong? I know how to cook. And these have been soaking since yesterday."

"No, no. X keeps running into things where something seems wrong to him. This time it's because be doesn't know the word 'mealies'."

∗ ∗ ∗

X sits up. Everything is dark, unfamiliar. Then he remembers – Nxele's house. The argument over whether the guest gets the bed. How he insisted that he was comfortable sleeping on the floor then wondered how he knew that. And here he is, awake in the dark, in a strange place – strangely comfortable with being on the floor.

But not totally comfortable. The voices are there again.

The signal is not strong enough to triangulate.

If only we had better equipment.

Somewhere between New Brighton and Zwide.

We can track the cop when his phone is on.

Can he hear us?

Maybe. Not likely, he is not fully functional.

To be safe, not too much chatter.

The voices stop. X resists the urge to join the conversation, something he suddenly senses he could do.

He gets up and starts pacing quietly – but possibly not quietly enough, as Nxele suddenly appears. "What's the matter?"

X repeats the snatch of conversation.

"Either you are seriously wrong in the head or these people are seriously after you."

"I do not feel safe in the city. It seems that they have some way of communicating that maybe is supposed to work for me, but they are not sure. If they can track me, they will find me. But if this thing has limited range, going far away make me safe from discovery."

A light goes on. Gladys's voice floats out of the bedroom doorway. "If you are going to wake me up with talk I might as well get up too."

Nxele says: "Ignore her – she wakes up pretty early and

is used to my early shifts." He turns on a light too.

X goes on. "Yesterday, when you had that robbery situation with a lot of cellphone chatter, it severely interfered with their conversation. So I am guessing it is something similar to the cell network. If I could go somewhere off the network for a while, maybe I would lose them."

Nxele contemplates for a while. "I am due a day off so I could take a long weekend, take you to my gogo in the Transkei. She is very rural. You have to go to the nearest hill to get cell signal. We could check if you really lose the voices in your head over there and it could be good for you to get away from the city to relax and get your memories back."

"Gogo?"

"Granny. What we call them up north. It is not a polite term down here."

"Aren't you worried about dumping a stranger with weird problems on her?"

"Believe me, my gogo can handle anything. The apartheid cops were scared of *her*. And anyway we will check how good your head's reception is and if you get the voices while I am there, I will bring you back with me."

The word *apartheid* sounds wrong: as if he was used to hearing it with a different accent but X lets it go. "I have no better plan. But why are you doing all this for me?"

"I love a good mystery and helping people who have a problem. Your mystery is one that I really want to solve. It is the sort of thing I joined the police for, not patrolling beaches and solving petty crime. My gogo may be very rural but she made me read from an early age – detective stories, science fiction, anything she could find cheap in second-hand stores. I sometimes used to think she only went to the city for that. Rural people have little money. So growing up with books is not usual.

"I was the first in the family who could have gone to university. She was determined that I should have the chance in life that she and my parents didn't have. She was disappointed that I joined the police – she saw me as a lawyer or doctor. But we did not have the money to send me to university. Back then, the government helped a lot less than they do now. I refused to let my gogo struggle to find the money. Policing pays OK if you are good at exams. I don't plan on staying a constable for long."

"What about your parents?"

"You really know *nothing* about this country. So many of us end up being brought up by our grannies. Our parents see themselves as failures and give up. My gogo taught me not to do that. I don't think she blames my mother for dying young but my dad – don't talk to her about him."

There is a silence. X senses a need to allow the subject to drift off. Eventually, he says, "How do we get there? Taxi?"

"No, no chance. It is a six-hour drive. There are long-distance taxis but you sit in them waiting until they fill up and sometimes they don't. I have a cousin who likes going out that way and is overdue for a trip. We will go with him. He is just waiting for an opportunity for someone to share petrol."

"Petrol?"

"Stuff you put in a car to make it go."

"Ah, gasoline."

"Right. It is about eight hundred rand each way. He needs help with that."

X says, "There, I can help. Happy to pay the whole cost. It's not like I am spending money on anything else."

"Don't be too hasty. You need food for the trip and more clothes. Then, who knows what? But if you pay half, which is a bit more than your share, that will be good."

The sky is lighting up fast. Gladys emerges from the bedroom and says, "We only have the one bathroom. If you need to go, please get it over with so I can get ready for the day."

X heads into the modest bathroom with a bathtub (no shower he notes) and toilet. The toilet looks unfamiliar. Nxele is watching his as he enters. "What's the matter? Toilet not to your American standard?"

"No. It doesn't look like the kind we had in Germany."

"Germany?"

X stands stock still. His head is in a crazy spin. "Yes ...Germany. I am not sure why but I remember being in Germany, spending real time there. I also remember that their toilets are very different to ours – American toilets."

"There you go, you are gradually remembering. And I also remember one thing: those strangers said they could track my phone. So I am leaving it off. I can use Gladys's phone to can call my cousin. And we can travel to my gogo without turning on my phone. So if you can just listen for voices in your head, we can keep ahead of them."

Gladys's head appears from the kitchen. "If you are going to take all day in there, rather take a break and let me use the bathroom."

"Apologies," says X. "I will not take long."

Shortly after, they are sitting around the kitchen table. Gladys offers corn flakes and instant coffee. She passes around sugar. Nxele takes a generous helping; X takes none. "Dd you always take no sugar in your coffee?" Gladys asks.

"I ...don't think so. Or, maybe when I was a kid .... Yes, my mom was a bit of health nut and didn't like sugar. Eventually she won me over."

"Don't you miss the sweetness?"

"I ...don't know." X looks distressed.

Nxele laughs. "Gladys my love, you made him remember something. But he is struggling with some strange things like remembering what things taste like. It is a big break-through that he even remembers his mother."

"The thing is, I remember I _had_ a mother – and this one little detail. I can't even picture her. Was she tall or short?

Long or short hair? Blonde or dark?"

"Don't worry my buddy. If little things come back when you don't think about it, maybe big things will too." Nxele turns to his wife. "My love, may I use your phone to call Mjolo?"

"What's wrong with your phone?"

Nxele explains the tracking issue. She looks at him wide-eyed. "This is not a detective novel. If there is danger, you should be passing this to the people in charge."

"They do not have the imagination to handle this. They would just send X back to hospital and those gangsters would be after him. It is not an easy story to believe but I am good at judging people and he is real."

"I am not so sure. I want you back in one piece."

X says gravely, "I don't know what this is all about, but right now he is the only person in the world I can trust. It is totally his call. I would not want him to take any risks that he is not comfortable with."

Gladys and Nxele exchange glances. X can see there is an understanding there that needs no words.

Nxele makes the call and says, "Right! We're on. Mjolo needs to pick up a few things in town, but we might as well go with him since you can also use a few more clothes."

"Back to Port Elizabeth? What was that other thing you called it that I can't pronounce?"

"No. There are shops closer to home in Uitenhage.

Smaller town that's part of the same metro. Gqeberha is the new name for PE. We don't use it so much when talking to foreigners. But we hope they will get used to it.

"Any voices?"

"Nothing specific, just the sensation I had before of noise."

Their ride, Mjolo arrives. He is more slightly built than Nxele, with a pencil moustache and a jolly manner. His car is dilapidated – it has an Opel badge and has a vaguely far-eastern look, a hatchback model completely unfamiliar to X. The engine however runs sweetly.

Mjolo leans out of the car window to stare at X. "My, bro," he says to Nxele, "who is this, the black sheep of the family?"

He and Nxele have a good laugh. X self-consciously looks at himself, as if for the first time registering that he is much lighter-skinned than his companions, a pale shade of coffee, indistinguishable from well-tanned caucasian, Arabic or mixed-race – "coloured" as someone said on TV news the previous night.

Nxele gets into the car and invites X in. "A long story – let's get the shopping out of the way and talk on the road. My buddy X needs some clothes and is a Woolies fan. I just need some *padkos*." To Mjolo, he adds, "As your first episode in the mystery, my new buddy has no idea who he is, hence X." He then notes the quizzical expression on X's face. "A bit of Afrikaans: *pad* means road, *kos* means food. So stuff to keep me going on the road. I keep forgetting you aren't one of our native whities."

"Afrikaans?" X pronounces the unfamiliar word with deliberation.

Mjolo looks incredulous. "Man, you are so ignorant. Afrikaans is the language of the Boer tribe who ran this place until 1994." He meantime has started driving and is manoeuvring around impressive ruts.

"As in Boer War?"

Nxele laughs. "You are *such* a mystery. You don't know you own name but you know about history from more than 100 years ago."

Shopping in Uitenhage is no adventure. Mjolo goes to buy food, with a generous handful of X's cash, while Nxele takes X to Woolies, which is clearly a branch of the same shop as they went to in the bigger city. He picks out clothes for sturdiness rather than style. A pair of good walking shoes, jeans, T-shirts, a few long-sleeved shirts, a few packs of socks and boxer shorts. After some hesitation, he also picks out a waterproof windbreaker. He looks quizzical as he browses. "Still feel strange?" Nxele asks.

"Very. But no different than last time. I'm also thinking: shouldn't we tell the hospital?"

"When I took you out, I was vague about when you would be back and it didn't trouble them. It's not as if you were arrested or a danger to the public."

They pay for the clothes and find Mjolo outside at the car. "Guys, I bought KFC for the road. And some refreshments for when we get there. Put your stuff in the boot."

X looks puzzled again then gets it. "Ah, the trunk."

Mjolo laughs. "Man, we're in Africa now. Only elephants have trunks."

"OK, but I think I know what KFC is. Chicken, right?"

As he stashes his shopping he stares at crates of large bottles filling the boot.

Mjolo shakes his head. "You know what KFC is but you don't know what beer is."

"As it happens I do know, but that looks like an awful lot of beer for two people."

Nxele claps him on the back. "For a start, it's three. We bought it with your money so we can hardly cut you out. Secondly, where we are going, it's a *long* trip to buy booze so we have to bring enough for everyone to party. Come on. You can go in front because I know the scenery."

They head out north on the N2, a decent piece of highway. X is starting to get used to being on the wrong side, though the way people drive seems chaotic. He turns to Nxele. "You're a cop. Explain the road rules to me. As far as I can tell, there are only two: too fast and too slow."

"Got it in one!"

They all have a good laugh.

"The sad truth is that the driving licence system is totally corrupt. Anyone can buy a licence," says Mjolo.

X turns to Nxele behind him. "Do the police have no pride in their work?"

"Some of us do. But we are not the main traffic enforcers. That is local government or province, out of the city."

"Province?"

"Eastern Cape here. We have 9 provinces."

"Ah, like states."

They lapse into silence as Mjolo makes good progress. Suddenly he slows as the freeway becomes a wide road with intersections.

To X, he says, "Colchester. Well known for a camera trap." Compared to their previous progress, they slow to a crawl. "Ah, there." He points at a nondescript grey box. "That looks like some sort of electric box, like we get around town. There is a speed camera hidden in there."

They immediately speed up – but this appears to be the end of freeway driving, with one lane per direction occasionally with an extra overtaking lane.

X loses himself in the rolling hills, sweeping valleys, huts dotted around the countryside, the occasional smarter house or government building breaking the pattern. Every now and then they see cattle and goats wandering around, mostly but not entirely clear of the traffic. Vehicles vary widely – from new, upmarket German cars to vehicles that looks as if they are held together with string and well-chewed gum.

Every now and then they stop for a refuel break, to take a leak or to polish off some of the copious KFC.

The sun is sinking by the time they turn off the N2 onto a short stretch of tar that quickly deteriorates to very rough dirt. Mjolo slows somewhat but drives as if his car was made for this, which it obviously isn't judging from numerous creaks and rattles. After about half an hour, they crest a hill to the sight of a clump of neatly-built modest-sized houses.

Nxele taps X on the shoulder. "My gogo's. She is a very strong person and you may need to learn how to talk to her. Wait here, while I tell her what to expect." They stop in a cloud of dust and skinny dogs run around the car barking. There are goats and cattle in the distance, and X sees a vegetable patch near the houses, protected by stout rough-wood fencing. Each house has a rainwater tank, and there is an outbuilding that he guesses houses a toilet.

Nxele strides energetically to the biggest house and an elderly woman emerges and starts talking sternly to him, gesturing to the car. Clearly, she has seen X so he opens the door and steps out of the car. He hears her words clearly but can't make them out because of the unfamiliar language with a variety of click sounds. The gogo stands with a slight stoop but gestures strongly as she talks. She is wearing a brightly-coloured orange dress wrapped tightly around her and a headscarf. Nxele motions for X to approach. He does so cautiously and extends a hand. "My apologies. I do not speak your language. I also do not remember my name so people call me X. I am told you are an impressive person."

She takes his hand perfunctorily and turns on Nxele again, particularly as the crates of beer start to emerge from Mjolo's car. She stalks into the house.

"Does that mean I am not welcome?"

"That is not the issue at all. She always harangues me because I wasted my talents and became a cop. You are just an irritation: she has never known any white person who was in her mind any good. She doesn't believe me when I tell her otherwise. So many families have been broken up by alcohol so she is not happy to see so much. But she will be happy when all the neighbours are here. Let's get your shopping and I will show you to your room. "

The room is small and minimally furnished, but clean. There is a bed and a shelf of books. X takes a look at the titles and fixates on the science fiction titles – Asimov, Heinlein, the old school.

Nxele notices that he is transfixed. "Another memory?"

"Yes. I know these authors. I can't remember when I read them though. Was this your high school reading?"

"My gogo wanted me to learn science but she bought anything that was going cheap. The fact that the word 'fiction' was there didn't trouble her too much. Reading this stuff I can tell you was a very unusual childhood. I would have had terrible teasing if I wasn't so big and strong. I liked reading about aliens and robots and androids, all that stuff."

X has another moment – but can't place the memory that is trying to surface and leaves it because there is another distraction: the sound of raucous voices outside. The neighbours have arrived. He goes out to find Nxele has preceded him and is being mobbed by around half a dozen young men who are shouting all at once and go silent as they see him.

Nxele makes introductions. "X, these are my cousins, the ones who are still trying to find work. There is nothing here except growing your own food and only the older people are into that."

Mjolo emerges from a nearby house. "Enough of that. The sun is going down. Time to party."

The beer bottles emerge. They are thoroughly warm from the car trip but no one seems to mind. A few bottles later, everyone is very keen to get to know X better. He tries his best but between their broken English and his broken memory, they do not get very far. After about an hour, everyone else seems to be rather plastered. He has not taken note of how much beer he has drunk, but he is not feeling any ill effects. As he is contemplating this, Nxele's Gogo emerges with a huge steaming pot of umngqusho and another of unfamiliar vegetables. Everyone is obviously famished and the food goes fast.

It is well past midnight when the party breaks up, and X finds himself alone in his room. It does not seem an

opportune time to ask about a bathroom so he strips down
to his boxers and goes to bed. The noises in his head are
completely stilled. He falls asleep almost as soon as his head
hits the pillow.

* * *

Light streams through the window. X sits up, shakes his head
to clear his thoughts and remembers where he is. The Gogo's
house. The wild party. He gets out of bed and feels rested.
Still no noises or voices in his head. At least that part of the
plan is working.

He walks outside and feels a strong urge to take a leak.
The outbuilding beckons. He goes over, pushes the door
open and sure enough, it is a toilet. At closer inspection, is
it is a raised seat over a deep hole. Still, the purpose is clear
so he uses it.

He walks out again, and finds the Gogo – he realizes this
has now become her name – striding towards the vegetable
patch. He walks over and greats her. "Gogo, good morning."

"Molo," she says curtly, which he takes as a response as
she opens a section of the fence. Inside, there is a bare patch
with a shovel next to it.

"Umlungu, uyazi yokusebenzisa ifosholo?" She is looking
at the shovel so he walks to it and picks it up.

With assertive instructions that he does not understand
and hand gestures that he does, it seems he is to dig trenches

around the unworked patch to match the patch where things are already growing. It is pleasantly warm and the physical effort takes his mind off his memory problem, so he sets to it with vigour, to her obvious approval.

She instructs him in like manner to add various layers to the area within the trenches – green leaves he does not recognize, the soil he has dug up, manure, dried leaves. On top of it all, she lays out old cardboard. After some progress, she alerts him to the presence of two large buckets and by verbal and physical commands makes him aware of a distant glimmer of water – at least a klick away. *A klick? Who measures distances that way?*

He turns and looks at the nearest rainwater tank. Her vigorous response indicates that there is no way in hell her good drinking water is going onto the vegetable patch. He turns and strides to the distant river, a round-trip of nearly half an hour. Despite his good physical condition, walking back is awkward as carrying two full buckets without spilling takes concentration. The Gogo surprises him by meeting him halfway back. She grabs a bucket and plonks it on her head as if it were a lightweight fashion accessory and walks back with him soundlessly, clearly making a point.

As they get to the garden, she removes the bucket from her head and shows by gestures that he must empty the water around the new bed. She turns and heads for her house, shouting loudly.

Nxele and a few occupants of the other houses stumble out, including Mjolo, looking the worse for wear.

Before anyone can say anything, two strangers appear from around the back of the Gogo's house. They have a resemblance to 'Fredrick Jones' – yet have a bland anonymity about them as if they could be anyone with blurred features. X feels a strange surge of both recognition and bewilderment and Nxele swaps glances between him and the strangers.

"OK, time we sorted out the mystery," says X.

Nxele rubs his head. "The biggest mystery is why you drank so much and look so fit and healthy today."

X stares at Nxele, a memory coming back. Andy is saying: *About the one thing I can think of that is not part of my daily life that's part of yours is ... getting drunk.* He alternates his stare with Nxele and the newcomers. "Droids ... Andy ... Heidelberg ... "

Nxele grabs him by the shoulders. "Heidelberg in Gauteng? What are you talking about? Droid as in android?"

"No. Heidelberg, Germany. US air force base, working with German scientists. We had droids, good enough to pass for human. *But this makes no sense.* I remember being a controller ... "

One of the strangers speaks up for the first time.

"You were a senior droid controller. A droid malfunctioned and exploded in your presence. We were able to transfer much of your memory to an android brain but before we could be sure it had taken, you walked out of the hospital."

Nxele looks suspicious, "A secret US government opera-tion in South Africa?"

"No, no," says the other stranger, "It was in Germany. We don't know how the commander – X – got to South Africa. We think he had help, That is why we have desperately been trying to track him down. And of course to complete the memory transfer."

X is struggling to regain his composure as memory frag-ments start to align. "Now, wait a minute. Something still doesn't fit. If this is a US government operation, why the clumsiness over the David Cramer passport?" Memories are stitching together thick and fast. "I've got it now. I was start-ing to suspect. There was a professor who spoke like an an-droid, the repetition of phrases as if he was one of them. You were getting too good at passing for human; you somehow were making droids with no human control... You had to elim-inate me, stop me talking."

The first stranger shakes his head. "No, no, it wasn't like that. Why would we restore your memories to a new body if we wanted to eliminate you? The explosion was a mistake. The base body ..."

"Yes, I remember now. Droids were sent to target jihadists, with a bomb built into their bodies – and some were becoming unhappy about being blown up and relifed into their base body, which wasn't supposed to contain a bomb.

How did they put it? *Disconcerting.*" The word echoes in his head.

Without thinking, he communicates without speech. *And now you want me back because something failed, some experiment didn't work. What was it? Relife me and tamper with my memories so I didn't know? Seems the experiment failed.*

That, it did, replies the first stranger. X suddenly realises that only one of the strangers is with him and the other has distracted the locals, who are now some distance away. X turns to the remaining stranger and asks, in a panic, knowing the answer: "Why is it only the two of us...?"

***

He feels warm. He opens his eyes, turns away from the harsh brightness, blinks. Then there is a shadow over his face. He turns to face the shadow and feels coolness on his back as it touches the bench – the bench he is lying on. His garment has a gap at the back.

He looks up to the source of the shadow. It is large, a not unfriendly dark face atop a strongly-built body. The body is clad in dark blue and is topped with a cap. There is a badge somewhere too; it is all too much and he blinks again.

He says: "How did I get back here? This is so *disconcerting.*"

The Empire Game

Kirth. Fourth planet of the Hundred Worlds of humanity. Dominated by the great continent of Krine.

Old enough to have its own distinct culture, its interstellar-class institutions, yet not old enough to be totally conservative and set in its ways. To many, Kirth, in the second century after the Expansion ground to a halt, the era of the Pause – the slowdown in the search for habitable worlds, the consolidation – is the jewel in humanity's crown.

In some ways, Kirth is startlingly Earth-like – a planet of vast seas, heady mountains, vast climate differences, yet a wide enough selection of temperate to subtropical regions to support a population of several billions. Its one spectacularly unique feature is a purple moon, so reflective that it casts a purple light even in daytime.

The Klavish uplands of Krine grow some of the Hundred World's best tea and coffee, while an asteroid belt is conveniently located for off world-mining, yet not so close as to constitute a danger to shipping. As with all but the first of the Hundred – humanity's home world, Earth – little vegetation or animal life on Kirth was developed beyond a very primitive level when the planet was colonised. While this meant that much had to be brought with the colonists, it also meant that there was relatively little to excite the interest of conservationists, who had put up a big fight for retaining pristine ecologies on newly discovered worlds, in the very earliest years of the Expansion. Unlike Earth, where the number of insect species alone possibly never would be fully catalogued, most other worlds so far encountered have species not running to more than a few hundred – possibly echoing the situation of Earth at the early stages of the development of life – though not as warm or high in carbon dioxide.

Some say this sparsity of highly-evolved life forms on new planets indicates that Earth is the first planet to develop intelligent life; others point to the vastness of the universe as indicating that intelligent life could exist out there and simply has not yet developed any detectable tachyon-based communication.

Krine, with an east-west spread matching old Earth's Eurasia and a north-south extent dwarfing that of Africa, holds a vast range of climates, from steamy tropics to icy arctic, and was the home of the biggest centre of population from the start. Even now that humanity has spread over most of the globe, Krine remains the most developed region of Kirth. While some other regions of the planet have developed a style of their own, Krine remains a cosmopolitan melting pot, where everything is possible, and no one takes themselves too seriously.

Contrary to predictions of twentieth-century SF writers, Earthly cultural differences hold little sway in the new worlds. Earliest migrants were highly individualistic, not the types to carry a little piece of home with them, and to attempt to re-establish inappropriate traditions. The very names they chose for their new homes – and sometimes themselves – emphasise their independence: often nonsense syllables that happen to capture a feeling a pioneer had on stepping onto strange soil for the first time. The language they speak on the tachyon to each other is an amalgam of Russian, American, Esperanto and Cantonese, with the grammar smoothed out, and what they speak at home is their own affair. Old Earth was forced to go along with the interstellar medium of communication, though many of the old languages persist on just that one planet of the Hundred.

The strongest Earthly influence is Universal Time, based on the old Greenwich Meridian and Earth's rotation and revolution, since planets with different planetary time need a common base to talk to each other about time and date.

With almost instantaneous tachyon communication, but no solution to the time dilation problem of relativistic travel, the Hundred are a strange combination of a closely knit community and a disparate collection of xenophobes. Yet somehow, it all works.

Every now and then, there is enough demand for some commodity on a distant planet that it is worth the investment to send a trading fleet out, despite the risks and costs of a journey lasting decades. For a tiny number of commodities, there is regular trade — but the sort of commodities where decades-long transportation delays are no obstacle. Exceptionally well-aged Earth Cognac. "New World" wines — a term borrowed from a different age of expansion — that are designed to age gracefully, the very best tea and coffee with an exotic tang of a distant world. And what better than interstellar space to ensure the freshness of vacuum-packed coffee?

With these commodities, whether the trickle of luxury trade or the odd spurt of large-scale commerce, a fresh band of émigrés move from one planet to another. But after the first outward rush of the Expansion, exploration has almost ground to a halt and each of the new worlds of the Hundred focusses on building itself up, not as a pale imitation of Earth, but as a new society of its own kind.

Tying all this together is a kind of loose confederation, a government by tachyon conference, in which the Hundred attempt to arrive at some sort of consensus on matters of general concern. Although Congress nominally legislates on all important issues, in practice, matters of local concern are always voted on the lines agreed by local representatives.

Considering that travel is such a problem and exploration has all but ground to a halt, the Confederal Government in effect has little to do but compare notes on local problems – but when something that threatens the Constitution comes up, it can act – as when Corbus came under the control of a fanatical faction that overthrew the government and attempted to take control of an unwilling populace.

Although it took twenty years for a fleet assembled from the three nearest worlds to arrive, arrive they did and, after restoring order, the plan was for them to stay long enough to ensure that the new government was not only stable, but had the means to provide for its population well enough to forestall any desire for another group of fanatics to grab control. Given the huge time loss resulting from near-lightspeed travel, many members of the fleet chose to stay on Corbus, rather than return to homes they would no longer know – so the plan changed to a permanent Fleet (now a proper noun) presence on Corbus, a warning to others who might have had pretensions of defying the Confederation.

But the Corbus Conflict is such a rare event that, even though it happened over a hundred years ago, it is still widely talked of as evidence that the Confederation really has meaning and is something more than a talking shop. Otherwise, many argue, why bother? If it were not that the Confederation is the guarantor of constitutional government on the Hundred Planets, it might as well not exist.

It is in this period of comparative stability and successful governance of human affairs on the Hundred Worlds that the Imperial Movement developed – as if there were those who would not leave well enough alone. Perhaps it is a characteristic of humanity that there will always be those restless enough to want instability – or perhaps those with a strong enough desire to be at the top that they would rather be at the top of a dysfunctional society, than enjoy equality in utopia.

Whatever the reason, it is not surprising, given that institution's illustrious history, that academicians at the University of Vala on Kirth are the first to foresee the problem.

* * *

Gravis Loomis, professor of antiquities, licks his lips nervously and looks about his office. Two or three centuries ago, it might have been lined with dusty books. Somehow, it still feels as if it were, even though the walls contain the standard view-screens, set to various portrayals of classical scenes, such as the Trojan horse, an Apollo spacecraft taking off and an early Earthly interstellar probe.

Loomis is elderly – getting on for 150 – and starting to disdain cosmetic rejuvenation, as an affectation of the wisdom of age. *In any case*, he thinks, *I have an indecisive chin and stupid teeth. If I look twenty, no one takes me seriously.* So his hair has a few grey streaks, and his face shows a few lines. He is slightly frail, as if having neglected his exercise in recent years, but nonetheless manages to sit up straight and throw off his feeling of nerves as he regards his colleagues and finds his voice – stiffening his chin involuntarily.

"I've called you all together, because I've observed some alarming tendencies in politics – tendencies that I fear that my reading of history indicates we are headed for serious trouble." He pauses to let the words sink in, and glances around the room to see that he has the others' attention.

"Our Confederation, having grown to 100 planets, is unwieldy to run centrally. While logic would seem to indicate a further loosening of the Confederation – perhaps a commonwealth or common market, if that concept applies with trade so minor an affair – there are some who are speaking with increasing emotion of the glories of expanding human space to create a Galactic Empire.

"In other words, they are talking about centralizing power even further, into the hands of some sort of Imperial Council, a thinly veiled excuse for suspending democracy. Their claim is that power is too dissipated in the current confederal scheme and no decisions get taken – quite the opposite to my view of the problem." He pauses again to look about.

"You all know of whom I refer?"

"Obviously," says political science professor Junes Divul,

"you refer to the Throgmorton faction." Divul, while almost as old as Loomis, prefers not to make an issue of her age, and looks pretty much like a fit 20-year-old, affecting purple hair to match the moon, a fashion of the young. She keeps her hair short in the utilitarian style popular this century and wears the plain black popular once again as a counter-culture statement. Loomis wonders how anyone could claim to be counter-culture while affecting more than one popular style, but suppresses the thought. In contrast to gender prejudices of the past, she looks more robust than does he; her rejuvenated looks signify the right to play the inconsistencies of youth, even if she is well over 100 years old. *And*, he thinks, *she has strong bones – everyone takes her seriously.*

Loomis nods. "Of course, this is all very much out in the open. So, I hope I'm not boring you with the obvious so far. The important point is not the obvious facts, but my analysis that I'd like to share with you, which, as I said before, contradicts the Throgmorton faction's claims.

"You see," he pauses for a bit again to gather his words, "every indication I have from past attempts at such highly centralised rule is that it only works for a limited time, particularly once the society concerned advances beyond a certain level of technology. Another important variable is the size of the overall society being controlled.

"For example, the Roman Empire pretty much held together, give or take pieces falling off the edges, and an eventual split into an eastern and western empire, for around 1000 years, and the last fragment, the Austro-Hungarian Empire, only fell after nearly 2000 years. If we look at this in terms of the population and territory involved, the Roman Empire was never particularly large by more recent Earthly standards – for instance, the British Empire. Also, the most advanced technology was little better than the lever, until the late stages of the Austro-Hungarian Empire, when the empire was long past its prime. Locomotion, for example, relied on human or draught animal power."

He looks around to see if he is boring anyone; it seems he is, so he goes on, speaking faster.

"More recently, the British Empire, the largest ever in human history, covered a quarter of the Earth's surface. Depending exactly on when you date its height, it lasted maybe 150 years – and came apart relatively soon after industrialisation started. A more recent example still is the Soviet Union, which came apart after about 70 years. It was far smaller than the British Empire, but it too was unsustainable under advanced industrialisation.

"Now," he again looks around the office, "my theory is this. There is a combination of factors, which may be possible to quantify, that limits the durability of any centrally controlled system. The level of industrialisation and the scale of the society being controlled seem to me to be the obvious factors, but I need some modelling skills that I lack to put numbers to these factors, and to extrapolate the model to the current situation."

Loomis turns to look out of a large window. The purple cast of midmorning moonlight never palls. His view takes in the university grounds and the way the moonshine picks out the colour of irises in the vicinity of his office is a highlight. *The unearthly emphasising the Earthly,* he thinks, but doesn't vocalise, as non-historians generally consider Earth to be boring as a topic of conversation – as he can see by looking around the room.

"Then what?" Divul seems unconvinced. "Whether this 'Empire' concept is viable or not, don't forget, someone has to push it through each planetary Congress separately, and eventually the Congress of the Planets. Somehow a 'Throgmorton for Emperor' campaign won't work too well – 'Emperor Throgmorton'? Doesn't have a ring to it. Aside from which –" she bares her teeth in a feral grin "– how would anyone enforce central rule on a widely-dispersed group of 100 planets, such as ours? I'm sorry my old friend, but 'paranoid' is the word that springs to mind."

Loomis looks at her levelly. "I suppose in the twentieth century there were people in Germany – if you remember your Earth history – who thought 'Hitler for Dictator' didn't sound like a likely campaign theme either. But he did not exactly run for office in that style – he whittled away at the institutions of state until there were none left to oppose him.

Putin did the same in Russia barely half a century later. I'm starting to see disturbing signs that the Throgmorton bunch are doing the same. Dispersed or not, we have institutions that rely on information from the centre, and that can be undermined."

"Like?" For the first time, the third occupant of the room speaks. Unlike the other academicians, Boon Jonx isn't a professor. He specializes in setting up complex models for groups such as stellar physicists. He could be Loomis's twin, but for his apparent age and the deep-set look in his eyes, perhaps a consequence of too much introspection about the nature of the universe, while steeped in modelling technique. Unlike Loomis, he has kept his youthful looks, and looks far younger than his 90 years.

Loomis replies, "Nothing too obvious yet, perhaps. But much detailed procedure in Congress committees has been delegated to task teams, the most important of which, con- veniently, are dominated by Throgmortonites. An increasing fraction of Congress business is rubber-stamping decisions of these task teams. And our beloved Congresspersons seem quite happy to have less to think about, and more time to chase after lucrative contracts. Once this kind of thing seeps down to planetary-level governance, we may find we have democracy only in name."

Jonx frowns. "This is all very tenuous – so what do you have in mind?"

"This. I would like to put together a model of the decline of past imperial societies, based on factors like population, geographic extent and technology levels, to see if we can come up with good predictors for past known empires. Then, we can attempt to predict the effects of an increase in centralization, even in the case of a minimalist libertarian government such as ours.   Once we have results of the prediction, we can decide how serious the problem is. I'd hate to commit to any action now, when it may be that a good model proves me wrong."

Loomis looks around the room again. "I don't think I'm asking for a big investment of your time – and there may be a publication in this even if I'm wrong." He smiles. This is the right button to push for an academician.

"All right," says Divul. "I suppose I'll go along, if mainly because I need exposure to this kind of modelling – I still think you're being paranoid. Boon?"

Jonx nods, his indecisive chin catching Loomis's attention, though unnoticed by the others. "I think I can find the time – more out of interest in the historical stuff. I developed an interest in ancient computing, so I already kind of have a foot in the history door. I'm also not at all convinced that anything big is happening."

"Good," says Loomis. "I'll provide the historical data. I'd love nothing more than to be proved wrong."   He turns to Divul. "Junes, maybe it would be best if you would dig up what you can on the current state of politics, since I'm really coming at modern politics as an amateur, and we can then help Boon with making a consistent model that covers both cases, the historical data where the know the outcome, and the developing situation we want to extrapolate."

He sighs. "In a way, I really do hope I'm just making a fool of myself. But I do have an uneasy feeling about what I'm seeing. I can't just let it pass without doing something." From the looks on the others' faces, Loomis can't help but feel they've already decided he is talking rubbish, but he suppresses the reflex to argue his case further.

They schedule a follow-up meeting and agree to keep in touch in the meantime on the net – discretely. After his colleagues have left, Loomis falls back in his chair and stares at his fingernails, his hands steepled on his desk. "If only I were convinced that I'm just a paranoid old fool."

* * *

Junes Divul squints against the bright light of the sun in the open air, a unaccustomed sight after weeks of reading through committee minutes. Jacarandas in full bloom cast a violet hue to the backdrop, as if foreshadowing the full purple of moonrise. She, Loomis and Jonx are snacking on bags of peanuts and dried fruit in the park-like grounds of the university, away from interruptions by students.

"Gravis, I must admit," she says, further shielding her

eyes, "I apologize for calling you paranoid."

The other two pause from their munching; Loomis looks grim. "Tell us the worst, Junes."

"First," continues Divul, "things are far further advanced than any of us could have suspected. Already, eighty years ago, Throgmorton, then a junior senator on Qwalve, his original home planet..." – she pauses to observe the surprise on the others' faces – "I thought that would shock you: not many people realise he has switched planets. But that's not all, he's done this twice. He was on Kirth forty years ago. Now that he's on Brax, we've taken note of him because he's openly pushing the imperial option."

She surveys her colleagues then goes on. "But consider this: time dilation works well for someone with a long-term agenda. Things he set in motion twenty years ago, even forty years ago are now playing themselves out, without his having to wait so much of his own subjective time. But I'm ahead of myself. Way back when he was in Qwalve, he led a faction that claimed to be in favour of stronger union, a tighter federal model. The movement wasn't strong, but they scored on one specific point: that there shouldn't be a repeat of Corbus. And the way to ensure that was to establish a Fleet presence at each planet, artificially replicating what happened by chance on Corbus: a corps of Fleet personnel who do not belong on that planet, whose role would be to ensure stability and constitutionality."

Loomis nods contemplatively. "I remember something about that – but it was all very unobtrusive. I think he managed to get interstellar Trade interests to pay most of the costs, since they were the ones who lost most heavily in the Corbus fiasco."

Divul smiles. "You are more or less right. The key point is 'unobtrusive': the general public didn't take much note of what was going on. When he was on Kirth, he took a few years to get elected again to public office, and pushed the programme on further. By that time, the Fleet presence was in place on all of the Hundred. His next step was to argue for a rotation of Fleet commanders, so no one garrison's leadership would be open to corruption by local politicians or commercial interests.

"Once again, he managed to get Trade finance for this – something that our remarkably naïve politicians and public opinion failed to see as an obvious conflict of interest."

"Yes," agrees Loomis. "I'm afraid even academicians are occasionally given to such lapses. I remember when that rascal Bloors fiddled equipment purchases..."

Jonx rolls his eyes at the mention of this as Loomis continues: "... and I was ridiculed as a troublemaker when I complained that he wasn't making the best decisions..."

They pause as a group of students wafts by; their youth somehow distinct despite rejuvenation technology making youth accessible to all.

"We digress," says Divul, "we aren't at the main point of my story yet."

The others clutch their snack bags and wait for her to continue. As the moon starts to rise, its reflected light purples the shadows – a sight unique to Krine's spectacular purple moonshine.

"Gravis, you remember you told me how functions of government were increasingly dominated by committees who delegate to task teams? That, it turns out, is not the start of the conspiracy. It's the tail end."

She pauses, looking at how the others are silently staring at her in shock. Not for nothing is Junes Divul considered one of the top public personas of a distinguished academy. *Definitely physical presence counts*, thinks Loomis. *Strange when we can be whatever we want to be.*

"According to my understanding," she goes on, "the committee system is designed to consolidate his position for a simultaneous takeover of power – but the underlying mechanism is not the committee system, it's the Fleet.

"You see, the conflict of interest is no accident, it's deliberate." She pauses again for dramatic effect.

"How –" starts Loomis.

She waves him to silence. "Though now I must start relying on conjecture – please hear me out. Imagine this: a select group of Traders has been convinced that trade is not going to grow without expansion. Yet trade takes so long to establish, with the long shipping times in interstellar trade, that to wait until the next period of natural expansion would be to wait for several lifetimes.

"So, these Traders have been persuaded that they can prolong their ground lives using Throgmorton's technique – slipping from planet to planet, relying on time dilation – while aiding and abetting his plans to force expansion under an imperial banner."

Loomis looks unconvinced. "I'm sorry, but this needs proof. I was the paranoid old fool before," he smiles, baring his stupid teeth then abruptly hiding them so as not to look foolish, "but now *I* want proof."

She nods and sees that Jonx also looks unconvinced – even though he keeps his teeth to himself. "So far, the only firm proof I've offered is of the obvious conflict of interest of the traders' funding of the Fleet and Throgmorton's apparently calculated moves starting with building up the Fleet, supposedly to protect the Constitution, and his current contradictory position where he appears to be undermining the Constitution. But there's more."

Again, the dramatic pause.

This time, Loomis is unamused. "Oh, get on with it Junes, this isn't one of your tachyon lectures to the entire known universe."

She lowers her eyes in mock apology. "So sorry. In the process of my investigations of the committee system, I chanced on a Trade lobbyist, who seemed to understand at once what I was looking for. At first, I was concerned that he was onto us and would block any further investigation, but he seemed as worried about developments as we are and offered to help dig up a few clues. He confirmed a few details but, most important, he was able to provide a few documents that led me to a trail of conspiracy – not very much, but enough to make it clear we're onto something."

Loomis looks gloomy. "If it's reached the stage where the conspirators are frightening their own, we may be in real trouble. Can we talk to this person? What exactly is your proof?"

Divul holds a hand up. "In time, in time. I need to talk to him again to convince him that he should spread this wider. In the meantime, I believe our best weapon is surprise. If we can achieve anything, it will be because the other side is overconfident but not quite at the stage where they're unstoppable."

All of them look around. Not even a student is nearby. *You would have to be truly paranoid to believe that someone is spying on us*, Loomis thinks, dismissing a vague shimmer in the air as a trick of the light. He sighs. "I hope you're right." He looks at Jonx. "Boon, what news on the simulations? Are you ready to put in current data? Are past empires behaving according to the proposed model?"

Jonx comes to life at the mention of his name. "Ah yes,

all this depressing talk – but I do have something to offer. I've set up models of all the old empires you gave me data on and have found the best fit. It seems that the critical parameter is the balance between communication and the ability to deploy force. If bad events at one end of the empire can't be communicated to the other in time for action to be taken, things fall apart eventually. How soon depends on how powerful technology is in general. The real big factor as I see it is that no empire, no matter how strong, can deploy sufficient force consistently over all its territory to put down a revolt. If there is no powerful opposing technology that can be used to deploy significant force, a relatively minor garrison can usually hold out even if communications are slow, until reinforcements arrive. On the other hand, even if communications are good, deployment of reinforcements becomes a major issue if the resistance has access to powerful technology, which could overwhelm even a well-fortified garrison in a short time."

He pauses to collect his thoughts. It's nearly moonrise, with a solid purple glow on the horizon.

"Communication is a powerful tool that cuts both ways: resistance to authoritarianism can also use communication to undermine central authority. This leads to authoritarian systems stalling their own development. Any civilization that aspires to rapidly advancing technology has to have an open, universal communication system. The Soviet Union, for example, couldn't sustain its development relative to the United States of America, when it did things like locking up copying equipment and seeing electronic communication as a tool of subversion. Putin, who tried to revive the Soviet empire, with delusions of being another Peter the Great, ran into this issue in another form. He tried to allow friendly propagandists unfettered access to social communication while shutting down others. All he succeeded in doing was to hasten his own fall when the falsity of his propaganda was overtaken by reality."

The full moon pops over the horizon, creating an illusion of dulling the jacaranda blossoms, even as its light highlights their colour.

Loomis looks thoughtful. "I wonder then what will happen when we put today's data in the model. We have very fast communication in the form of the tachyon, but deploying reinforcements is a very slow process. On the other hand, would our people be up to employing weapons of mass destruction against the Fleet? Could they, given that the Fleet's main force is in space?"

Jonx nods. "I'm keen to put all this into the model."

"Right," says Divul. "No more guesswork. I'm looking forward to putting some science into the problem. Meanwhile, I'll try to persuade my informant to open up to all of us."

*　*　*

Hamish Empree is heavyset and dark with nervous, quick movements. It is as if he is watching for spies in the shadows – though none in the coffee shop are deeper than the shadow in which he sits.

Junes Divul walks into the coffee shop and squints into the gloom in various directions, as Empree is nowhere obvious, then hurries to his spot after finding him in the darkest corner. "Hiding?"

"If you know what I know, you would be more cautious."

"Please share." She takes a seat facing him, with her back to the entrance. She notes that he has a nearly empty cup already and asks the servitor for her own.

Before the emergence of Divul's drink, Empree starts, with an air of urgency. "I am concerned that they are onto me. I have asked a few people questions that have had them raising eyebrows, so we really do need to be careful. Watch your back. What I am sharing now has them nervous and making the powerful nervous is... risky."

Junes shakes her head. "We aren't living in the twenty-first century, with players like the Chinese with spies everywhere."

"Don't be so sure. I am sending you some passkeys to critical documents. Be careful how you access them, so it doesn't get back to you. Or me." He drains his cup and stands up.

Before Divul can say anything, she has the passkeys on

her interface and he is gone, leaving his now-empty cup looking lonely. She barely notices when her fresh, steaming cup pops out onto the table.

* * *

Divul has a taste for ornaments – statuettes in various materials, placed strategically around the office to break its utilitarian monotony. None of this registers because of the shocking event that has brought them all together.

She stares around her office grimly. "You have all seen the news. By now, you may have guessed that Hamish Empree was my contact. Dropships do not routinely crash on takeoff."

Her pause is less for dramatic effect than to ease the tension but what she has shared has the opposite effect. Noticing this, she speaks briskly. "We need someone with good skills at securely accessing documents without leaving a trace, to read what he shared with me. Boon, you're the techie."

Jonx, already looking concerned, becomes even more so. "My further work on models suggests that they must strike soon if at all. I am not really an expert on secure document access because academicians usually don't need that, but I work with students who have those skills. I will inquire discreetly. More seriously: can they link Empree to us, Junes?"

"I really don't know. I only met him twice. Once was a coincidence. The second time, after we shared innocuous messages about meeting for coffee, I saw him for a minute or two. In a coffee shop. Unless they are onto my digging... but why would they be? We are only academicians. Digging is what we do."

Loomis looks around the room, catching each person's eye in turn. "Paranoid. This is the time to be paranoid." *What was that vague shimmer? Surely nothing but a trick of the light. Moonshine is notorious for that.* Loomis keeps the thought to himself.

"But, in practical terms, if time is running out, we need to get the proof fast, completely... and go public with it without delay. Are we all agreed?"

Every head in the room nods.

"But," asks Divul after a silence, "who can actually act on it? Planetary defences are minimal because the Fleet is supposed to guard against a rogue planetary government."

* * *

They are meeting out in the open again. A group of academicians taking a snack break in the sun, once again, to all appearances, celebrating the full glory of a mid-morning full moon – as are many others. To the observer, nothing would be untoward, except that none of them have opened their snack bags.

Paranoid... thinks Loomis. *With 100 planets to spy on, surely no one would even think of eavesdropping on an insignificant group like us...* he drops the thought.

"Two things..." Jonx breaks the ice. "I accessed the documents, and they absolutely confirm our suspicions. I will share copies now. Check your interfaces. This should be secure. I accessed them with an ID of a non-existent academician from Blaine. If anyone was eavesdropping, they would start looking on a distant planet. You all have more expertise in the politics than I do so I will focus on my model."

Jonx shakes his snack bag but doesn't open it. "As we surmised, they are close to seizing control but the weak point in the whole thing is communication. Since we can spread tachyon messages throughout the Hundred including the Fleet, we can undermine their plans by something as simple as spreading the truth."

Loomis nods. "That works for people on the ground. What about the Fleet? Junes, you are more in touch with modern political thought. Would Fleet personnel be loyal to people on the ground or to Trade?"

Divul looks thoughtful. "They all have a home planet. They may not have much affinity for people on the ground where they are stationed but they would have some loyalty to family on their home planet."

After some discussion they all agree. They will put together a tachyon presentation showing the undeniable proof of the plot and broadcast it to all known space, including the Fleet.

"Three-dimensional chess." The others look puzzled, so Jonx explains. "You win by ensuring that the other side plays in the wrong dimension. Throgmorton and his ringleaders are playing a long game against Ground using time dilation. We will play in all-of-humanity communication. It will isolate him. Instantly. Thanks to tachyon tech."

In a more optimistic frame of mind, they all open their snacks while discussing the details and agree that it should be done without delay. Jonx nods. "I can set it up as soon as you have the content ready."

There is a vague shimmer in the air again but this time none of them notices. They part with a new sense of purpose, confident in their strategy and that they have surprise on their side.

A cloud crosses the moon, changing the vista to one of plain white light of the sun, that somehow looks brighter when in fact there is less light without the moon's purple reflection. *Illusion. Such a human weakness.* Loomis yet again keeps the thought to himself.

* * *

After the tachyon broadcast goes out, reports flood in of citizen concern from all of the Hundred and numerous Traders deny complicity. In short order, the Traders' Guild issues an

official statement denouncing any form of coup and commit-
ting to the Constitution.

They all converge on Divul's office as it has a view over
the city, much higher above ground than Loomis's, allowing
them to see residents clumping together in animated groups
to discuss developments.

Loomis looks triumphant. "We did it. The conspiracy will
never take off now. It is all out in the open."

None of them notice the stranger just inside the door until
he speaks up. "Not so fast." They all look around in surprise.
The stranger is slightly built with red hair and looks to be
about 20 years old though with much older eyes. He has a
strange moustache, bare in the centre, cut short on the sides.
The opposite of Hitler, it seems to signify, thinks Loomis,
though, to the non-historian, this would be obscure, so he
holds his silence. The newcomer is flanked by two others,
both heavily armed.

"But I forget my manners. Let me introduce myself.
Vannevar Throgmorton. You will know my name from...
how silly of me, it is your very own tachyon broadcast."

Everyone stares at him in bewildered silence.

"You see, rejuvenation technology and time dilation work
very well for those with a long view. I am 300 ground-
years old though, to me, only 80 years have passed, and this
plan started a lot longer ago than you realise. Once we had
shielding technology to protect spacecraft at such speeds

and a practical way to accelerate to near lightspeed, it was just a matter of time before someone thought up a plan like this, I thought. But, surprisingly, I was the only one. Which is what makes me the leader.

"Fleet is entirely comprised of old Traders who started out in the very early days with me, long before we were at 100 planets. We have all employed time dilation and rejuvenation to work on a very long-term vision, in the full expectation that humanity would stagnate. Virtually no one in the Fleet has living relatives on the ground who they can relate to. Most of us have been in space at least 200 years, ground time."

Throgmorton pauses to survey his audience and his tone changes. "Well done on your analysis but you missed a key fact."

His gaze around the room holds them spellbound. Those old eyes in a youthful, freckled face with hair in the spiky style affected by rebellious youth looks so disconcerting. Then that weird moustache... this is a person who wants to be noticed. And remembered.

"It is *all* of Fleet that is in on the long game, not a small cadre of conspirators."

"Rotating the commanders...?" interjects Jonx.

Throgmorton looks triumphant. "Aha. That was a ruse to cover up the fact that the main personnel also have no loyalty to Ground. So Fleet as a whole has no loyalty to anyone on the ground. From now on, this empire is run from space and will grow humanity in a way that none of you can even conceptualise. In my empire, Ground humanity has one purpose. Supplying the Fleet so we can expand our reach. We will recruit from those who support our vision. Otherwise, to us, you are irrelevant."

"Traders...?" asks Loomis.

"Most are not in the know. They will be with us or no trade. This will ensure that we get what we need – even if only a minority of the Hundred comply."

The academicians nod in unison. This explains the Guild's stance.

Throgmorton continues: "No play, no pay. We have the only guns in space, to put it crudely. I would be sad if Krine was cut off. The best moonshine in known space, both the purple light kind and the purple booze named after it. But needs must..."

The purple light outside catches a glass ornament on Divul's desk in a way that exactly captures the look of the best Krine Purple Moonshine as he says this and Throgmorton glances that way before continuing.

"You have no way to project force in a way that is mean-ingful so I very much hope that Ground humanity will coop-erate. There are good practical reasons to build the Fleet in space and we used that as a pretext to avoid building a major armaments industry on the ground.

"My needs are modest for plans of vast scope, but I

cannot have foolish parochial interests thwarting me. We will seed humanity on new worlds that will appreciate my vision from the start. So, if cooperation is not all I want it to be, we will simply leave the Hundred behind – though for now we do need some ground-based resources."

Divul breaks the silence from the academicians' side. "So, what are you going to do to us? Are your goons going to throw us out of a window, like Putin's thugs? Empree..."

Throgmorton's wide grin is somewhere between humour and predation. "Oh no, nothing like that. And anyway, you forget. I am on Brax. A virtual presence is not going to throw anyone anywhere. You as masters of the tachyon lecture should know..."

Jonx slaps his forehead. "Tachyon 3D! But this is far better than any we do. No flicker. No translucency. Not using equipment on our side. But now that I look closer, your backdrop lacks the subtle purple light of the rest of the room."

Throgmorton looks even more triumphal. "Ah, the techie. That's a small taste of how far Fleet is ahead of the Ground Hundred. And that's why we don't need to behave like savages to get our way. What was done to Empree was clumsy. There was no need and those responsible have been disciplined. Clumsiness is not my way. He – and you – have no comprehension of how advanced and unstoppable my plans are."

Loomis breaks in: "Corbus..."

"I'm sure you are working it out as we speak. You're a bright bunch." The Throgmorton grin again. "Totally engineered. We landed an armed group that stirred up trouble. In a population unprepared for that, we took control easily. Then I solved the problem that I created myself by building a Fleet. Which won easily with minimal bloodshed because the intervention was up against my very own goons, who didn't want to get killed."

Loomis nods grimly. "The self-created problem. The easiest kind to solve, provided you have worked it through to the solution."

Throgmorton surveys the room, as if inviting questions. No one has anything to add, so he continues. "I admit a certain lack of originality. Putin did much the same thing in the 21st century in his Ukraine war but with abhorrent clumsiness. It did not take academicians such as yourselves to see through him. Unlike him, I have a very long view and am subtle about creating conditions for success. I appreciate intelligence and initiative even if I will not allow it to hinder me. I am here to congratulate you for trying."

Still no response from the room.

"But you failed. I am your emperor now, and there is nothing you can do about it."

Following a dismissively imperious wave, Throgmorton's retinue vanish, leaving him alone in the doorway, apparently about to vacate the academicians' presence too. Throgmorton pauses. "In parting, let me add: I miss your purple moon so perhaps someday I will be back..." Then there is a more pointed pause as he adds: "Oh, and one more thing. Three-dimensional chess. You're absolutely right that the dimension I played in is time dilation. What you missed is: it isn't just me and a select group who have broken all connection to Ground, but the whole Fleet. Your tachyon broadcast had the exact opposite effect to that you intended. It triggered the entire Fleet to activate our carefully-designed plan to take control of critical resources on each of the Hundred. Before anyone could mount any form of opposition. So, I am also here to thank you. But don't expect any statues of yourselves. The moment is mine."

Emperor Throgmorton the First grins smugly at the academicians' stunned silence.

How could he know? Three-dimensional chess came up in a private conversation in the open air – the shared thought needs not be vocalised. His tachyon image winks out, leaving only a vague shimmer. Remembering what Jonx said about *no equipment on our side*, Loomis points at the shimmer in horror. Then, it is gone.

Don't Look Back

Another bright, sunny day. It was great to be out in the open with dirt on his claws. Professor Spines dusted himself off. The dig was looking exciting. The great bones were starting to take shape as soft sedimentary rock chipped away. His students were enthusiastic, which helped a lot. He had to pause every now and then to dissipate heat, a problem that escaped youth.

One of them was shouting.

He lumbered over. "What is it, Amber?"

She was pointing at a bright, sparkly spot around one of the smaller fossilised bones. He peered closer, and she chipped away more.

He stood up. "Remarkable. That almost looks like pure gold. I wonder how it became wedged there."

"Not wedged, professor! It goes around the bone."

He took a closer look. She was right. It looked like an artifact. An artifact in an impossible location. "Keep taking photos. We'll need to record every step."

He drifted off ... This couldn't be right. There was no intelligent life 110-million years ago – unless this specimen was much more recent. But that would be wrong too. Skeletals had never been intelligent. Not those little *furry* things that lived on the fringe of the modern ecosystem, those little *scaly* snakes and crocodillies that hid under rocks in swamps when they weren't kept as cute pets, the furtive birds, that kept out of the way of everything else – and surely not *this* primitive giant. It couldn't be substantially more recent. There was the Coal Gap. 8-million years when coal formation stopped. There simply was not that much life on the planet over that whole time, and no fossil record of giant skeletals after that. And the rock they were excavating had only recently been exposed by geological processes. What a conundrum.

Amber was shouting again. Didn't that grub of a girl realize he needed to *think*?

He sighed and ambled over. She had cleared more rock. What he saw took his breath away. Despite erosion over time, it could only be an artifact. A ring of glittering gold.

* * *

That night at the camp fire, the professor had them gather round.

"This is a great day, we've made one of the greatest finds

in history." He looked around the fire-lit circle of glittering eyes. "Not hyperbole. This is something fantastic. For the first time, evidence that we aren't the only intelligent life forms that ever lived. To purify and work gold requires significant intelligence. The ability not only to work with fire, but to achieve extreme temperatures, maybe even chemical skills."

He paused for emphasis. "Of course we will need to do the hard work in the lab to date the specimens. But there is very, very little probability that this life-form is less than 110-million years old – or that its descendants existed much more recently than that."

Scarlet put up a hand. "Professor, you mean the Second Die-Off?"

"Exactly, thank you Scarlet. Both Die-Offs resulted in around 90% of all living creatures, over 70% of all species, disappearing. Then, each time, after about 8-million years, the two great Coal Gaps, when not much life above the yeasts existed – nothing big enough to decay and form fossil fuels. Nothing much big for 8-million years. Just enough left to restart the system. Do you all remember when the First Die-Off happened?"

Turquoise offered an answer. "360-million years ago."

"Very good, Turquoise. And what did the two great Die-Offs have in common? Amber?" Time she had some limelight, after her great discovery.

"Anoxic oceans."

"Great. Caused by?" he prompted her.

"Big rises in CO_2."

"Excellent. And why are we sure of the CO_2 link?" Another prod. Amber must know this.

"Because it's the common factor between the two Die-Offs."

"Good work, Amber. And of course some of the lesser die-offs may also have shared some of these factors. But what is strange about the Second Die-Off?" He looked around the ring of students. Turquoise was keen to talk, so he gave her the floor.

"No obvious cause."

"Excellent. We had natural causes like orbital changes, volcanoes and evidence of meteorites for the other extinction events, even the lesser ones, but the Second Die-Off? Just evidence of a sudden uniform world-wide spike in CO_2 – no evidence of massive volcanoes, no evidence of a big meteorite strike. And why should that worry us today – if I am a bit off topic?" Spines eyed out the group. No one offered to opine.

"Never mind. A pet obsession of mine. Let's all party. A celebration of our great find, and Amber's good work."

They scurried for their packs, secreted honeybeer suddenly acceptable to consume openly.

Such great gals, he thought. Always trying to be the best,

none at all fazed by a male teacher.

＊

The audience was restless. The end of a long hard day, many boring speeches about well-rehearsed topics. Paleontology, as one of them joked, was not something where you could expect something new.   And repeated the joke at every meeting to emphasize the point.

Spines stood up, and advanced to the lectern.

There was a rustle of anticipation. Despite keeping his silence about the topic, his excitement – his students' excitement too – could not be contained. But he started sedately enough, flicking through title and introductory slides.

We all know about the two great Die-Offs: the anoxic oceans, the strong connection between the two of a massive spike in CO_2 levels, the conversion of the seas into hydrogen sulfide factories.

We all know the conventional wisdom that it was the Second Die-Off that was the eventual impetus for intelligent life, the clearing away of life-forms physiologically unsuited to high intelligence – the great skeletal monsters – leaving our distant ancestors a clear field.

The audience became restless. This was not something exciting... not yet.

So, Spines continued, *I have a discovery that could change all that.*

He stopped talking and slowly flipped slides from the first glitter of gold to the uncovering of the whole circle of gold. Thin and pitted though it was, in the slide it looked very clearly like an artifact – one which had probably been worked with some accuracy, though this was hard to see in the slides.

The room became entirely silent, but for the murmur of a fan.

Spines allowed the moment to develop, then produced the artifact with a dramatic flourish – as dramatic as he could manage with its weight – its scale suddenly more apparent, a fragile gold band the size of his hand.

Pandemonium.

When eventually the room quietened down, he pressed on.

What is especially remarkable is that we found this thing around a bone of an extremity of a skeletal fossil that must have been at least 110-million years old. He stopped and glared around the room, waiting for someone to contradict him. No one did.

And here is a reconstruction of the entire skeleton. His next slide revealed a stooped bipedal form, big eye sockets in a domed skull, its fore-limbs lightly resting on the ground. He switched to another slide with him standing next to it, its vast bulk clear, as it towered over him, at least four times his height, even with its stooped posture.

As we can see, the skull is enormous, though we've found

skulls from ocean-dwellers that were even bigger. This one has space for a brain of almost one-and-half litres, about double the size of ours. We know of course that our brains are of a more complex internal organization than surviving skeletals, but none has a brain anywhere as big as this fossil would have had. So it is at least plausible that it was intelligent.

At that point, he did have an interruption. A delegate from the front row whom he recognized from previous conventions spoke out. "You mean to say you think that *thing* made that artifact?"

He contemplated for a moment. He didn't know her name. She never talked to him. Perhaps deliberately, now he thought about it, with that attitude. "Yes. Yes, I do. Perhaps you have a better theory?" he asked levelly.

She glared at him. "Yes. I think a male in a female career is thinking with his pheromones."

Some but not all of the cries in response were in his support.

* * *

Unusually for a paleontological conference, the media was there in force. Spines's revelation had spread exceptionally fast.

As he left the auditorium, Spines was still shaken from the insulting riposte. *After all these years, who would have thought it? I've always done good work. I'm not a raving masculinist or anything, but* ... and he walked straight into a mêlée of shouting journalists and TV crews.

"Do you really believe skeletals could have been intelligent?"

"Show us the artifact!"

"How old is that thing?"

He waved for silence and slowly, reverently produced the gold ring. It was scarred and pitted and barely connected in places, but still showed evidence of craft – too round to be random.

The journalists stared in silence, the reality of the thing more shocking than any indirect hint that it may have existed.

Eventually, he spoke, choosing his words carefully.

"This thing was around an extremity – I cannot think of any better explanation than that it was wearing it. Gold is a soft metal but not very reactive. It must have somehow been shielded to have lasted that length of time – perhaps in a soft spot in the sedimentary rock that didn't cause much friction as the skeleton fossilized and shifted over the millions of years."

One of the journalists asked, "How old ... ?"

Spines said, "If this thing is less than 110-million years old, we will have to rewrite the entire book on paleontology – not to mention geology."

Another asked, "How are your colleagues taking this, I

mean *you* finding ..."

"I know what you mean," Spires said grimly. "Males should stay at home looking after the grubs."

"I didn't ..."

"Well, some of my colleagues did. I had some pretty insulting comments back there." He gestured to the auditorium. "I thought we were over that sort of thing in this day and age. I'm not a big campaigner for male rights, I just feel that I should be judged on my achievements. And anyway, one of my students made the big find. It's as much a slight on her as on me to belittle this find because of who I am."

He wrapped up the artifact and pressed through the crowd, refusing all further attempts at interaction.

* * *

Spines tumbled onto his sofa. The television was already on though no one was watching. Pearl was doing her turn at the house chores, another example of their semi-liberated household. The curved outer wall gave him comfort, the feeling of being in his own space. He rolled over towards the screen, some of the tension gone.

He was just in time for the news. The lead story was his exit from the convention.

"Pearl!" His wife came in, followed closely by their youngest, Ruby.

Ruby was in her early post-metamorphosis, her adult

features fully formed, but with the awkward look of a tween – the moves not quite right.

Spines patted the sofa, and they collapsed onto it next to him, in time to see him barging into camera.

Ruby was staring wide-eyed at the screen. "Wow, dad. You're a hero. I wish I was a boy."

Her parents laughed.

"Too late for that, dear." Pearl tingled her daughter's back spines. "We can't change the choice we made before cocoon. And anyway, you're wonderful the way you are."

Spines shook his head in agreement. "Believe me, if you like the work I do, you want to be a girl."

The news switched to the interior of the convention centre – background from the other delegates. The interviewer cornered one of the other scientists. One who was only too familiar to Spines. "What do you think of a male making the great discovery? A turn-up for social attitudes?"

The scientist grimaced. "You are assuming it's a great discovery. And anyway he didn't discover it, it was one of his students."

"So you don't think even scientists are ready yet for male equality?"

"When males prove they are our equals, we scientists will accept that evidence. Until then ... "

"You mean you don't think much of Spines?"

She clenched her mandibles in frustration. "Am I not

getting through to you? He has a totally emotional approach. That gold thing he found – *if* it's gold – could have many explanations. He has jumped on one. Cranial capacity isn't intelligence – otherwise the giant sea-skeletals of that same era would have been super-intelligent. Yet they were all wiped out in the Second Die-Off. No evidence of artifacts from them."

"What other explanation is there?"

"It was his dig. He has the evidence. How am I supposed to evaluate the range of possibilities? He probably wrecked the evidence in his hurry to get the thing out. Emotional male. Hmph."

The camera switched to the interviewer. "There we have it: Professor Spines-ka Pearl is an emotional male, and this whole thing is of no significance. If anyone should know, it's Professor Emerald."

Spines smacked his head. "Of course!"

"What, dear? Had an emotion-driven inspiration?" Pearl goaded him playfully.

"No, no. I should have known who it was. I never paid much attention to who was who at our meetings. Social convention. No males to talk to so I keep to myself outside sessions. But I've read plenty by Emerald. She does great work in her field, but has published a few rebuttals of mine, always snidely worded. Doesn't really understand my stuff, outside her area, but if you're a Name, you can get away with it."

He slumped into the sofa.

At that moment, Jem came bounding in. Two years older than her sister, she was becoming quite athletic, and was on the school's first qenja team. Spines smiled at the enthusiastic physicality, quite unlike his own bumbling youth.

Jem snuggled up to him. "What's this I hear, dad, about how you are some sort of news sensation?"

He snorted. "Trust the TV to blow it up. But I think it may be something quite big. You know how it's conventional wisdom that we are the first intelligent life form to evolve – at least on this planet?"

She nodded.

"I was on this dig with some of my students, and we found this artifact, a circle of gold around an extremity bone of a fossilized skeleton."

"Dad! Why didn't you tell us?" Ruby demanded. The two kids nudged him playfully.

"No tickling!" They subsided. "I really didn't think you were that interested. I used to talk about the latest dig and everyone would doze off."

"But this is different! Evidence of intelligent skeletors! Just like in the SciFi stuff. I can't believe it." Jem stared at him in mock annoyance, all eyes focused on him.

"Skeletors?" her dad enquired.

"That's what we all call them at school. What would you call them?"

"There were thousands and thousands of skeletal beings in the past, possibly millions of types – we can't be sure because the fossil record is so patchy. Up to 110-million years ago, they may have been the dominant large life-forms. We can't call one of them something that could apply to all of them – though we will need a non-scientific name for popular consumption, now non-scientists are talking about them."

"Wow. 110-million years. How old was that thing you found?" Ruby's eyes were all focused on her dad too but in awe.

"Not likely to be less than 110-million years old – almost all skeletals died off around then. We still need to do some work to date it accurately."

Jem pressed the point. "What *do* you want us to call it?"

"Well, the official classification is based on a combination of approximate age in millions of years, approximate brain size, number of legs and a few other numbers for the bone structure. There's supposed to be a common name as well, though no one has named this thing yet, though lots of fossils have been found in the past, because it's never been a subject of popular attention. This one comes out as skel-110-1500-2-556."

"Skeletor it is."

Jem was definite on that point, so he nodded. "You know, I do have naming rights, and I haven't come up with a popular name, so skeletor it will be. Even if the scientists won't like it." He paused. "Let me give them one more thing not to like, now I've started."

"What about the gold thing, dad?" Jem was not giving up on chasing the details.

"Museum. I'll have to take you to see it. It will be a while before we can put it on public display. Meanwhile, what have all of you been up to? Jem, how did the qenja go?"

"Great game, dad. Even if everyone thought it was a bit odd that mum brought me. Can you take me next time? Please?"

He looked guilty. "Of course, of course. I don't want my work to turn me into a bad parent."

Jem and Ruby were all over him. "Bad parent?" He couldn't tell which was talking. Maybe they both were, echoing their thoughts. "Dad, you're a hero." To them, he thought, Emerald's sneers still echoing in his head. Cranial capacity. Anyone could tell she didn't think a male's cranial capacity counted for much.

* * *

The great head with its vacant eye sockets stared at him. Spines sidled up to it slowly. He put a claw-tip on the skull, chitin to bone-fossil, and stared into the eye sockets.

What had its eyes looked like? Would they have been the yellow slitted things of modern-day crocodillies? The pale shiny things of a fish? Of course those are aquatic creatures. What, today could be similar?

Nothing, obviously, in terms of intelligence. Nothing with a skeleton, anyway. He'd never seen a spark of intelligence looking into an eye of one of the children's pet dillies.

What did this creature know? Certainly the ability to decorate itself with gold indicated not only an ability to work metal but some sort of artistic sense.

Did it know poetry?

Did it know the sweet smell of a fernflower?

Did it revel in the heady flavour of a sweet, frothy honey-beer?

Did it know love, hatred, the pleasure of seeing ones off-spring metamorphise and convert from weak, helpless little things to creatures of intelligence, initiative and personality? For that matter, how exactly did that happen? Did it produce eggs like a modern reptile? Or did it produce young that went through a metamorphosis as we do? How did a big head develop after exiting the mother?

Did it appreciate the senseless complexity of something like the game of qenja?

All his eyes remained locked onto the empty sockets, until he was interrupted by a rustling.

He turned from the stooped skeleton. "Sorry, Jem. I still

can't walk past it without wondering what sort of life it had."
She followed him silently into the curator's office, the solem-
nity of the moment not lost on her youthful consciousness.
Some quiet words passed between Spines and the curator,
who found a large bunch of keys.

"Follow me." The curator led them down a dark passage-
way to a strongly made door. "Most valuable finds in here,
I will have to stay with you." Not that I don't trust you, she
seemed to say.

The three of them filed into the dusty room. The curator
reverently lowered a heavy box from a shelf. She opened it.
Inside was the gold artifact, and a thick wedge of notes.

"May I touch it?" Jem had a few eyes on each of the
grown-ups.

Her dad looked at the curator, and they both nodded. Jem
reached out a claw delicately, and caressed the pitted metal.
"110-million years," she said softly, the only sound breaching
the silence. The dust lay heavy over the room, emphasizing
how nothing should be disturbed in this place.

They all stood there several minutes in silence.

As they turned to leave, the curator reverentially repacked
the artifact and notes and stowed the box, barely disturbing
the dust.

Back in the exhibition hall, Spines and daughter paused to
examine the skeleton. He pointed out how the bones seemed
to indicate a fairly upright stance.

Jem looked puzzled. "How could it balance on only two legs?"

"We don't know. Maybe it ran like that, and rested on its forelimbs. Maybe it straightened up briefly to see long distances. Could have been a survival thing – that's what we used to think before this evidence of intelligence. A wild creature like this would have had an advantage if it could see over high plants for example."

"Did it have scales like a dilly?"

He smiled. "There's no way we can tell. All we have is the shape of the bones – at least for this variety. It could have been hairy, or scaly, or had feathers." He laughed at the expression on her face. "There were many, many different skeletals in their era. The few today may be rather unappealing creatures with ragged decorations and coverings, but who knows what they may have looked like when they ruled the planet. They may have been magnificent. The few where traces have been left indicate scales and feathers were very common. We can't be as sure of hair because it doesn't fossilize. But we have to guess one of the three from the few skeletals still around."

She looked unconvinced.

"Come on." He led her away. "Let's go to my office and I can show you some of my stuff. You did say you wanted to do my kind of work."

"Ooo yes."

They left the building and after a short walk through shaded fern groves arrived at his office.

The room was cluttered with samples and tools – mallets, hammers, rock chisels. She gazed around in wonderment. "Dad, you play with girl's toys."

"Now, don't you start." He quickly steered her to a batch of samples. "Look at these rocks. Look closely."

She stared, all eyes focused on details. There was a lacy pattern which resolved itself into a feather. "Wow. What was this off?"

"Don't know for sure. We think it may have been a very lightly boned skeletal. Some people think it could fly."

"Fly? With such heavy bones?"

He laughed. "The bones near this feather were extremely thin. We can't be sure because they were fossilized but we think they may have been hollow – no heavier than your arm shells.

"Take a close look at each of these – I just want to check for messages – so many after that TV thing."

She nodded, engrossed.

He tapped on the screen. As expected, a slew of messages popped up. The summary lines mostly looked uninteresting ... then one popped out and demanded his attention.

Did skeletals mine coal?

This may seem radical but I think you should

```
investigate.  I work at a coal mine and we
found a whole lot of skeletals before we got
to the main coal.  And the mine started as
an iron mine - a few tonnes of high-grade iron,
mixed in with skeletals, then coal.  Something
really strange going on.

Interested?
```

As Spines took this in, Jem turned to him. "Dad, I was going to ask how I get to study this stuff but you look like you saw a ghost."

"Something I have to deal with. But Jem: if you take my advice, don't look back. Get a career that looks forward. To the future. To things we can't do now."

***

The mine was a hive of activity. As the airship approached the landing dock, Spines saw workers scurrying too and fro, dwarfed by giant machines. There was a black dust over everything, visible on the tops of the buildings.

So that's why they call it Black Mountain...

When he alighted, Diamond stepped forward and grasped his forelimbs formally.

"Professor. So glad you could make it. I know academic funds are limited. There are a few things here though that are very hard to convey without a site inspection."

"No apologies needed. I was glad to be able to get away for a bit. Not," he added hastily, "that I want to get away from *family* ... work pressures ... "

Diamond laughed. "I can imagine. We get even fewer male geologists than there are male professors. But when I tell you what I've found here and my other thoughts on the matter, you'll see there is stronger cause for ridicule than being the wrong gender." She looked grim by the end of the last sentence, humour evaporating under the harsh glare, as they walked towards the mine workings.

She led Spines to her office, a prefab building, fans battling to maintain an even temperature. Spines had to splay out his wing case to let some air in. Diamond indicated a chair. "Make yourself comfortable. To the extent that that applies here. Mining is a dreadful business. Always dirty, dangerous – usually in some queen-awful place, terrible climate. Water? A little honeybeer? I have a stash kept cool ... "

"Thanks. But I had some on the airship, and need to keep my head clear. Let's get to it ... not impolite or anything, but I want to see the cause for excitement."

"Of course." Diamond unrolled a large sheet of paper, a site plan. Spines watched closely. In his profession, he seldom saw paper in quantity. "Let's spread this out and pin it to a wall."

The two of them worked on the paper, Diamond less

clumsily, obviously accustomed to such manipulations.

"Now," Diamond pointed at the paper, in its new role as a poster, "look closely. The red lines represent the extent of the original find, which as I told you in my message, was high-grade iron. You'll see that ends abruptly, and the green line represents the extent of the coal reserves as we expect them to exist starting from the early dig." She pointed out of the window. "You can see that we've dug up about 10% of the reserves so far, and they are a good fit to what we expected."

"With you so far. Explain the big surprise."

"Look at the border of the red and green areas. You can see it's almost a clean cut."

"OK. But I'm not a geologist. Is this unusual?"

"As it happens, no. But what is strange not only here, but in many other cases, is that the geology model we've built up is very reliable in maybe 50% of the cases. You see, if we hadn't found iron here and had instead found the coal from the other end, there is nothing to say the coal should have ended abruptly there."

"The iron ...?"

"Yeah, well that's the really strange thing. The geology suggested there may be coal around, but the first thing we found was this really high-grade iron. So we started an iron mine. Around 100 tonnes later, it was all gone, and we hit coal. All wrong, not the right geology for iron. And why such high grade? You would get that maybe if you buried near-pure iron for long enough for it all to oxidise. And very lucky conditions, so it would stay there. As it happens, the site here is surrounded by nonporous rock and has been geologically stable for over 100-million years."

Spines nodded. "And the skeletals?"

"Only in the area where we found the iron, not mixed in with the coal. That was a bit unusual. If I understand fossilization right, they would have had to be buried in mud, and the area above was in fact probably under water."

She paused. "That's why we called in another palaeontologist, a specialist in marine fossils."

They sat down, facing each other over Diamond's desk.

"Oh?" Spines enquired.

"Professor Emerald."

"*Emerald*?" he barked out.

"Uh, yes, Emerald ba-Rock ... "

"I know who Emerald is. I doubt there's another professor Emerald in palaeontology, common though the name is in high society."

"Some history?"

"Sorry. She was rude to me over my finding."

"Ah, yes, as seen on TV. Forgive me. But anyway, she dug up some molluscs, little marine skeletals or whatever was interesting of that era, then hit hard rock and skeletals, big ones, probably similar to the one you dug up, said there was nothing more interesting, and told us to carry on."

"Nothing more interesting?"

"To her. I asked about the skeletals, and she mentioned your name, and said she'd get back to us if you were interested, and that was the last we heard of it."

"How long ...?"

"Oh, that would be about five years ago."

"Damn! All that lost evidence." Spines looked resigned. "Your information is interesting in itself, I suppose. But we can't read too much into one example. Even if this wasn't all lost, how much would it add?"

"Exactly. That's why I've been doing a more detailed study. You see, there's this inconsistency in the geology. We think we have a good model of how coal is formed. But about 50% of the time, as I mentioned before, we're wrong. In a fair number of cases, the coal is weirdly truncated, like this. I don't know if skeletals are found in close proximity in other cases."

"Well, fossilization is hit and miss. You have to have the right conditions. And even then, you have to be incredibly lucky to make a good find."

"Right." Diamond nodded. "That's what I thought, so I decided to take up another line of investigation. I looked for another differentiating or common factor. And ..."

Spines leaned forward across the desk.

"... all the truncated finds have been in rock formations that would have been near the surface for over 100-million years. The non-truncated finds are mostly in areas where the geology would have raised the surrounding material significantly through tectonic shifts within the last 100-million years. A few are areas that would have been buried deep underground, or under sea 100-million years ago."

"Any exceptions?"

"None. None so far. Not of the truncated ones, anyway. A small fraction of the untruncated coal fields may have been in accessible places in the distant past. There is always some uncertainty in dealing with the deep past."

"Have you told anyone this?"

"Actually, it's not that hard to find this stuff out. The facts are already widely known. The mine geology texts all estimate coal finds as 50 to 100% higher in areas elevated in the last 100-million years. It's just a matter of taking note of the fact, and wondering why. The texts say 'for unknown reasons', which is a bit of a cop-out. You work through all the theory and add a fudge factor that has no basis in theory."

Spines put a forelimb on Diamond's back, a gesture of surprising affection among strangers. "Take my advice. You may not be a male, but if you tell anyone else about this without hard, *really* hard evidence, you will be treated like a complete idiot."

"You mean, you ..."

"I mean I know what it's like. I think you may be onto something, but there's a lot of people out there who don't want to know."

"Emerald?"

"Like Emerald. But leave her to me. I'll have to think through how to deal with her."

"Let me know when you have more ideas. Meanwhile I'll keep plugging away on my evidence. Uh, and professor..."

"Yes?"

"I stopped looking at oil geology when that made even less sense. Oil needs very specific conditions to form and to persist for millions of years. After we started working that one out, we only had rich finds in about 20% of the places where the theory said it should have been."

"Meaning?" Spines felt a chill through his wing case.

"Meaning I stopped working in oil and shifted to coal." Diamond ground her mandibles. Spines touched forelimbs formally, and turned to leave.

* * *

Back on the airship, Spines was shaking.

Confirmation. But would Diamond take his advice and shut up? Well, she had kept extremely quiet about the oil thing. So unsettling. But one thing at a time. And that one thing was bad enough.

Sometimes, it was better not to know.

That damned Emerald.

But the truth was out, and would eventually have to be

taken into account – at least by the open-minded. Skeletors were intelligent. They worked gold, they mined coal. They died out abruptly. Coincidentally – or was it so coincidental? – they died out after a rapid spike in greenhouse gas emissions, a rapid poisoning of the environment and an abrupt climate change. Surely they could not have caused this themselves. Our own civilisation is starting to cause severe environmental degradation, but nothing on that scale. Impossible. But so was a skeletor who worked gold.

It all sounded so SciFi. No, better that Diamond should shut up for now. At least until more evidence could be found.

Or ... until someone confronted Emerald.

He set his mandibles.

I think I know just who is going to confront Emerald.

* * *

Once again, Spines only felt comforted when he could slump in his very own sofa in his own home. That wretched Emerald. She may be a legend in marine palaeontology, but she had no right to block him like that. Five years! How much time had he lost because she had blocked him from that dig? But could anything there have matched the gold artifact?

Suddenly the kids were all over him. Jem, her athleticism evidence again in her rapid bounds into the room, Ruby not far behind. Pearl brought up the rear, laughing at the scene. "I hope your students don't treat you like that. You'd never survive more than two of those."

He smiled grimly. "Students I can handle. That damn Emerald."

"Emerald again? She wasn't at the mine?" Pearl sat on the edge of the sofa, pushing Ruby aside to make space. Ruby squeaked indignantly.

"Not now. Five years ago." He explained what had happened.

"The cockroach!"

"Ruby, I will not have foul language in my house." Pearl looked very stern, and her daughter wilted.

"Sorry, mum." She didn't look sorry, quickly recovering from her parental chastisment. Spines patted her head. An understanding passed between them.

Pearl failed to head this silent communication, and focused on Spines."So, my dear, what are we going to do about her? We can't have her obstructing your career right and left."

Spines contemplated for a moment. "Let me think. Maybe I should get you all dinner. It will help me clear my head."

In the kitchen, he savagely hacked at vegetables, the feeling of dealing out violence surprisingly satisfying. He assembled a stew of various roots, leaves and fruits, with herbs thrown in for good measure. While it simmered, he helped himself to a honeybeer, and called out, "Drinks for anyone?"

With a honeybeer for Pearl and a couple of nectarjuices

for the kids, he went out to see what they were up to. A science show was on. It was about evolution, how skeletals had once ruled the earth. He stood transfixed, until he heard something boiling over, and scuttled back to the kitchen, back to his properly male role.

As he passed the food around, Ruby asked: "Dad, do you think the skeletors really ruled the world? I mean, built machines, had civilization, and so on?"

"What did they say on that show that I missed while I was in the kitchen?"

"Old stuff. Nothing about your work. Dinosaurs, elephants, when crocodillies were big and ate animals." She grimaced.

He laughed. "Not like your pet, dear. It's tiny. Those big monsters would have been a hundred times the size."

"Why are they so small now then?"

"We think after the big Die-Off, only very small forms of skeletals survived. Our own ancestors were much smaller, but more adaptable. When life came back, the skeletals, the few that were left, couldn't adapt fast enough, and the big forms never came back. Pushed out by our ancestors."

"That reminds me –" Pearl broke in – "someone hasn't fed her pet."

Ruby grumbled as she got up and went to her bedroom.

"Dad," Jem finally managed to get a word in, "didn't some of the other land skeletals have even bigger heads than our skeletor?"

"That's true. Elephants were enormous. But the area we think the brain was in was not that big. Some of the sea skeletals may have had big brains. But since we have no idea how the brain was structured, we don't know if they were intelligent or if for example the big brain was specialized for sense of smell."

Pearl looked thoughtful. "Can't we learn anything from current skeletals?"

"Of course. But they are so little, and there are so few of them. It's unlikely they would have preserved the range ..."

There was a shriek from Ruby's room. They rushed there.

"It *bit* me." She was standing over the crocodillie's hutch.

Spines took her arm and examined it. "Barely a scratch, dear. It must have thought you were a dry twig."

She eyed it out suspiciously. "You know our lot wiped out your lot, don't you."

The dilly slowly blinked an inscrutable yellow eye, and casually slurped slime from its trough, as if nothing had happened.

* * *

This is it. He looked up her connection details and set up the call. The screen pixellated briefly as the stream was set up. She recognized him.

"What do you want?" she asked brusquely. "I don't imagine you think I am going to apologize for telling things the way they are."

Emerald was obviously a hard case. "Well, a little civility always goes a long way."

"Hmph. If you put two and two together and get five, what do you expect?"

"Better than putting two and two together and getting zero."

She looked puzzled. "What do you mean?"

"Black Mountain colliery. Five years ago."

"Oh, that. I suppose you're going to make a big thing of it." Emerald looked at him with clear distaste.

"No, no. I just think we would do a lot better working together, not against each other."

"Me? Work with *you*?"

"Well, we *do* work in different areas. Your work in marine palaeontology is excellent. I don't want to intrude in that in any way. I'd just like to compare notes on a few issues, like the two great Die-Offs."

"And if not ...?"

"You mean would I make something of Black Mountain? No. But look: what would it cost you? You have your reputation. All I ask is a few minutes. I can go to the marine paleo symposium at your campus next week. If you can fit me in for a few minutes between sessions ... "

"Well, all right then." She looked as if she was having surgery without anaesthetic. "Against my better judgment.

Just don't make a fuss about it."

"I haven't made a big thing of the other things, and I am not going to start now."

"Hmph." She broke the connection.

He felt weak. But he'd done it. No backing out now. He went to look for Pearl, out in the garden. She was clipping at a cycad tree. He collapsed onto a bench, and she came over to him. "Not accustomed to the female job of fighting battles?"

"Actually, no. But I think I am getting used to it. But the hard part is ahead."

"Oh?"

"She agreed to see me. I'm going to her symposium."

* * *

The moment of truth. This was it. At some point not too far in the future, he had known he was going to confront Emerald. In truth, though he had relished the thought at the mine, he wasn't so sure now. Emerald was a formidable marine palaeontologist. The symposium was not quite in his area, but he was nonetheless interested, so he sat back and paid attention – *let the science do its work: calm me before the storm.*

The break between sessions was only a few minutes. Emerald led him to her office in grim silence, the mere fact of having him there an admission of defeat. The cool comfort of the campus felt more like a sombre chill than it should. She opened the door and ushered him in. The curve of the walls didn't offer the usual reassurance of being inside a place that was shaped like home.

He pulled himself together, as she turned to face him, a desk between them as they sat down.

"So," she began. "What do you want?"

"Just to talk, to share some ideas. I'd like to know what you found at the Black Mountain site."

"Well, it was a nice marine sediment site – a shallow sea, probably not under water terribly long, a hundred thousand years at the outside. The whole lifetime of the sea must have covered a period around the start of the Second Die-Off plus or minus a million years."

"And?" He leant forward in his chair.

She shrugged. "Most of the fossils in the sediment were smallish skeletals, a few shells. Quite typical of the late skeletal era."

"Nothing particularly interesting?"

"Well, the thing that would have placed it right at the end of the late skeletal is that there was evidence of elevated carbon dioxide in the sedimentary rock. We know the late skeletal ended with a CO_2 spike, which endured for thousands of years, short on the geological time scale."

"And under the marine layer?" Spines was getting impatient – she was skirting the issue.

"I knew you'd insist on going there."

"It was you who told Diamond you were going to refer that to me." He favoured her with a pointed stare. "Was there anything interesting there?"

"Well, the CO_2 enrichment ended as soon as we got through the layer with the most recent terestrial skeletal bones, which indicates they would have died at or around the time the CO_2 levels started to build."

"Anything else?"

She slowly, reluctantly opened a drawer in her desk, and produced a shiny piece of metal. It wasn't gold, but somehow it was reminiscent of the gold he'd found – but a less complete piece. At his reaction, she said, "I know you are going to get over-excited about this."

"And that's why you suppressed this?"

"Well, you would have added two and two and made five."

"So you said about my other find. In any case, this one is *your* find. You need not have referred it to me." He sat back and contemplated her. "You were afraid of your reputation, that someone like you would ridicule you, just as you ridiculed me. Weren't you?"

Her usual composure wilted, but only slightly. "Look at this thing. It's barely possible that it's an artifact. I am not sure if I believe it is one myself. I saved you making a big fool of yourself – then you go public with that other *thing*."

"You did, did you? If you had even tenuously supported

me and suggested following up on my finding – even without mentioning this flimsy evidence – you would have risked others doing what you did at the conference, wouldn't you? So to make sure, you got in first. Forgive me if I am skeptical of *saving* me."

She nodded unconvincingly.

"But you see," he went on, "that's not the only option. I quite agree with you that this piece is really nothing to go on. It looks plausible that it's an artifact, but I wouldn't have gone public with it. I would have searched further. Compare this with the thing I found. Is it really the same thing? This one could have been a piece of a perfectly formed circle. But the fragment is too small to be sure. Did you take a close look at the thing I – my student – found?"

"Not really," she admitted grudgingly. "I admit it looked more plausible than this thing."

"So look, I am not asking you to abandon any deeply held principle, change your work to suit me or anything like that. All I ask is that what I do is taken on its merits. And I would really, really appreciate it if you could at some point in the future free up some time to talk me through some of the more complex aspects of your work. There are some things about the great Die-Offs that are not completely clear to me, that a marine perspective would aid in understanding."

She glanced at the time. "All right then. I will do my best to hold myself in check, as long as you don't talk rubbish. I am certainly not going to back you in any absurd conclusions based on inadequate data. I think we should be getting back now though, the next session is starting soon."

As they headed back, the conversation with Diamond haunted Spines. What would Emerald have made of *that*? Not only artifacts, but evidence that the skeletals were big miners of coal? Nope, best to keep quiet. And the oil thing, even more so. For now. And had she agreed to future meetings? Not exactly. But she hadn't said no, either.

* * *

His office has not been abandoned long enough for the dust to settle. The lights flicker on and the clutter is in its familiar place. The comfort at being back is punctured by a shadow crossing the door. It is the department chair, Professor Opal.

Opal pushes her way in and closes the door. She looks anywhere but in his eyes. "A lot of people have been concerned about this craziness of your supposed artifact. Some have been proposing that we fire you, but your other work has been good and let's face it, we are a liberal university and do not want to appear to discriminate against a male."

"And if a female made such a discovery..."

"Well one didn't."

Spines thinks of his student and decides better of saying anything.

"To avoid further embarrassment, we have decided to

offer you a special early retirement package. You will get your full salary until your usual retirement date."

"Emerald? Did she ... "

Opal senses his anger despite his measured control and cuts the thought. "No, it did not come from her. We did solicit her views and she was the one who argued for the early retirement package rather than dismissal."

"I see. And this is your measure of 'liberal'?"

"Please don't make this harder than it needs to be. We are being very generous. Your feelings ... " Her words blur into the sound of a career being trashed and excuses that try not to sound anti-male and mentioning anything but pheromones while meaning exactly that. All he gets out of it is that he'd better not resist as the package on offer is sweeter than fighting the system and losing.

Not liberal at all; my best option is to shut up and go.

He holds back the urge to tell her to stop matronising him.

* * *

I can't relate to being a househusband. I was a moderately distinguished professor until I became an extinguished professor. But my daughter is an astronaut. I can be proud of someone. I was disgraced without good cause but I can be vicariously proud. My other daughter is an artist. I can be proud of that too though, as a scientist, I don't understand her art.

So I cook and clean. And watch the news. And get invited to exhibitions I don't understand, but at least the snacks are good.

This is me.

I turn on the news.

Our first mission to the Moon is the breaking news. I wonder why as it is still many months in the future. I pay attention. This is Jem's world; she is on the list for the first landing.

I am still watching when Ruby bounds in, energetic as ever. "Dad! Neglecting the housework as always! Do you want me to do the washing up so you aren't in trouble with mum when she gets home?"

I point at the screen. There is a close-up of something on the Lunar surface, something indistinct – but shiny.

"Dad, what's that?"

"Jem's mission to the Moon, if she is selected, pushed forward as early as possible. It's an impossible artifact, something made of shiny metal. Big enough to get a photo from lunar orbit, not big enough to see clearly from that distance." I correct myself. "A shiny patch? An artifact? No one is sure. But nothing else on the moon is shiny like that so what else can it be? The orbiting probe's camera doesn't have enough resolution for a clear image."

I leave Ruby to stare at the screen. She's right, I have neglected the dishes. And I need to prepare supper; even if I have been dismissed as a professor, I can still be a competent househusband. I don't want her help, not now. She needs to take in the new story. I have the gist already, even if more detail – no, speculation – is unfolding as I head for the kitchen. Ruby is too engrossed to object.

* * *

Three years ago. I am in the Dean's office. The department chair's offer of an early retirement package rankles. But appealing to the Dean makes no difference.

"Did you really think your department chair could make that offer without reference to me? In fact, it did not even come from me. It came from the top. The university cannot afford embarrassment. It is actually out of my appreciation for your previous good work that I negotiated a generous early retirement package."

Chastened, I empty my office of everything that's mine. Though I wonder if anything that relates to academia is worth the effort, I take everything home. I have a study at home that is not yet full and my househusband duties surely can't take up all my time.

* * *

Back to the here and now. The phone rings. It's Jem. I grab the phone, dripping dish water as I go, before anyone else can, somehow sensing it is for me. "Dad! Have you seen the news?" I turn on video though I don't need to see her to know how excited she is.

"That I have," I reply. "Are you on for the Lunar mission? They're saying it's happening sooner than scheduled."

"I don't know but I am pushing hard to be on it, and I more than qualify."

"Good lass. You know I will be proud of you no matter what."

As I put the phone down, I hear the front door open. Pearl is in the kitchen in rapid strides, almost beating me to the dishes. Pearl opens with: "Have you seen the news? Everyone is talking about it."

"Absolutely, I only abandoned it to do the dishes."

"Ah. Would that be why the phone is wet?"

"Guilty as charged. The phone rang and, as I guessed, it was Jem."

"Is she on...?"

"Not yet," I reply. "They haven't announced the crew yet. But she's confident that she's in with a strong chance. And of course, the Moon mission has been pushed to top priority."

"I see. Will that happen so soon that we don't get to eat tonight?"

"Oh! I am a bad househusband! Will all the excitement, I forgot to cook."

Ruby snaps off the news. "Come on! Let's go out for a change and celebrate! Our Jem is going to the Moon!"

"Very probably..." I start.

"You're such a scientist! You can never be certain of anything! You know she's the best!" Ruby pushes me towards the door, her bemused mother in tow. So going out, it is.

* * *

Things move fast. The media keeps the story live and the Moon mission is preparing far faster than anyone had expected. I worry that the danger will increase because of the rushed timelines. Jem phones. She can barely contain her excitement. "Dad! Are you the only one who picks up the phone?"

"I'm the only one who has no career and can afford to skulk around the house."

"Oh. Do I have to tell you again how sorry..."

"No. Forget all that. I want to hear from you. Are you definite for the Moon crew?"

"Yes! That's why I am phoning. And I am actually so glad that I am telling you first."

"Me? Because..."

"Why? Because it may yet vindicate your crazy theory."

"The stuff that got me all but fired? I'm sorry, but the high-ups who pushed me, pushed me really hard. I don't foresee a 'sorry' at the end of that."

"Never mind. I always believed in you, and still do. I saw

the evidence with my own eyes. No way is that anything but what you said it was. Listen: we have to go into isolation soon. Can you tell the others? I am not sure if there will be time to talk again."

"Of course. But tell me: the way they are rushing it... safety..."

"Oh, dad. Trust you to think of that angle. Of course all the safety issues are being observed. But some things can be sped up by doing more than one thing at once. I promise, it will be as safe as if we went as originally scheduled."

I am still staring at the phone when Pearl gets home. "What's the matter? Has a ghost phoned?"

I snap out of it. "The opposite, I hope. Jem is in and she has gone into isolation with the crew, so that's probably the last time we talk until after the mission. I very much hope to have her back here and safe to tell us what she sees."

Pearl holds me close, a surprisingly juvenile gesture. But I don't mind. This is a special moment. Sadly, Ruby is away launching a new exhibition so she can't share the moment; it will have to wait until tomorrow.

I pull away and look closely at Pearl. She is the same Pearl who made her vows so long ago. "Come on. You had a hard day's work. Sit down, and I will make your favourite dinner." Just this once, I am in the mood to househusband.

***

When Ruby gets home, it's a bit of an anticlimax. The crew is already old news – only a day after the announcement. Things are moving so fast. She joins me on the sofa, watching the latest update. The rocket is being readied, with massive fuel pipes being connected, in time for the launch tomorrow.

A voice intones: "Fuelling happens at the last minute, as some of the chemicals are so volatile that they can't be loaded until they are ready for use."

I turn to Ruby. "That isn't super reassuring. Our Jem will be on top of that thing."

Ruby gives me a stern look. "Since when has Jem been the one to worry about? You got yourself fired. Even if it wasn't technically being fired. I do crazy arty stuff. Jem is the rational one, always super-prepared."

"I suppose you're right. But having lost so much, I couldn't bear to lose one of my daughters." My turn for a stern look. "You had better keep safe too."

"Oh, dad. The worst than can happen to me is falling off a ladder, and I haven't done that... often."

That lightens the mood. I get up. "Come on, I hear there's a qenja game over at your old school. Why don't we watch? I know it is more Jem's thing, but it will be like old times."

"Dad, you're such a romantic when you try. Who would guess you used to be a scientist?"

I let the painful 'used to be' pass. I stay in the moment. My older daughter is an astronaut and will soon be on the

Moon. My younger daughter wants to watch qenja with me. Life could be so much worse.

And – who knows? – my crazy theory could be vindicated in the most spectacular way possible. If that shiny thing on the Moon is in fact an artifact, how did it get there, and when? We have not had capacity for space flight until very recently and have not landed anything remotely close to that spot on the Moon. Or so they say on the news.

The game is heating up as we get there and Ruby looks around the pitch. "I still don't quite get why this excites anyone. It looks like pointless complexity to me. And I am an artist, and 'pointless' according to the critics is my thing."

"That's mean. I don't understand your work, but that's my fault, not yours."

"Nonsense. Art is for the viewer, not the artist. If mine is not for you, that's nobody's fault. Someone else will get it. And probably dismiss stuff you like. Anyway you're ducking the issue. What do you see in qenja? You being a scientist and all, a creature of logic and order."

Not 'former'... I take the win. "Logic and order for me are work. The crazy illogic of the game is a release. And besides, Jem enjoys it, and I loved to be with her while she was having fun."

"Mph. Do you love watching me work?"

"Actually I do, but it's harder to show pleasure when I don't understand. For all its illogic, qenja has rules that I can make sense of even if they seem silly. I understand it, even if I can't play. Just trying to make sense of all the variations on when the ball is in play is pretty tricky – even if it fits a clear set of rules."

There is a loud yell from the pitch. The referees have just finished conferring and all toot their horns in unison, confirming an extra penalty, putting the home side clearly in the lead.

"Look at that, Ruby. Cheating gives you no advantage. If only it was like that in real life."

"What do you mean...? Oh, your work. Your bosses there are such *cockroaches*." I stay silent and don't admonish her for the slur.

We watch the game with no further comment. The home side is racking up points; the visitors are clearly not up for further cheating, having been caught out.

We watch until play breaks off, and we are about to set off, when I realise that one of the home players has approached. "You're Professor Spines, aren't you?"

"Was," I admit ruefully.

"I just want to say that what happened to you is so wrong. If I have a boy when I have my own family, I hope he grows up in a fairer world."

I am about to say something when she goes on: "You must be so proud of your daughter. I hope whatever she finds on the Moon vindicates you."

Before I can respond, she is gone. I turn to Ruby. "Of course I am proud of both of my daughters."

"Dad, Jem is the one in the news. It is her moment. Let's not elevate my daubings as if this is one of those juvenile contests where everyone wins a prize."

I think better of arguing. My daughters may be more behind male liberation than I am, but they still have a way of dominating me.

$$* * *$$

The phone rings. I don't answer; Jem is unlikely to be calling at this hour, with intense training on the go, and who else calls our household for me?

I hear Pearl talking animatedly and ending with "Yes, yes. But I am not sure if he..." She calls me over. "It's media. They want your comment on Jem and the Moon mission."

"Do they now?"

Despite misgivings, I reach for the phone. A voice at the other end sounds vaguely familiar, perhaps someone I have heard on the news. I decide not to ask because I am not interested in popular culture and don't want to embarrass myself.

"Is that Professor Spines?"

"Former." Video is off, I note. It stays off.

"Of course. There is talk that the find on the Moon could represent ancient artifacts. What do you say?"

"I say you should talk to a professor how hasn't been prematurely superannuated."

"Ah. But you were the one making claims of ancient artifacts, many millions of years before intelligent life is generally agreed to have evolved."

"And no one took that seriously."

"Also, your daughter in on the crew."

"Ah. So you are trying to get at her through me. Sorry, no jenqa. No foul." I inadvertently break into the language Jem used to use at school and shake my mandibles to clear my head, glad that I did not take the call on video. "Now look, she has made a career of her own. Whatever you or anyone else says about me, she should only be judged for who she is. And that is a pioneering astronaut, something she achieved for herself – and that has nothing to do with me."

"But the find..."

I cut the connection and turn to Pearl. Her look is clearly approving. That matters to me a lot more than anything anyone watching the news believes. I ask: "Did I say anything that would jeopardise Jem's place on the mission?"

"Of course not. As you say, she should be judged on her own achievements. And even if she owes more of that to you than you admit, she would be proud of you if she saw how you handled that. As am I." She points at the door. "Come on, let's get out of the house. I know a place you like to go out to."

* * *

Launch day. It's live on the news. There have been other missions but landing on the Moon was not meant to be so soon. Almost everyone on the planet must be watching, but none with the keen interest of our household. Our Jem is on the crew. And no matter what denial I may be nursing, so is my reputation.

We have a zoomed-out view of the rocket – as we must, to see such a massive artifact. The news commentary drones on for those who have not been following previous reports.

"The main stage is to get the crew into orbit. Once there, the crew module separates and docks with the smaller transit stage to accelerate to the Moon. That was previously placed in orbit."

A tiny spec appears in the distance, and resolves into an open vehicle, with four figures evident. The crew. There is no way we can identify Jem at this distance, but the screen shows close-ups of each face in a row underneath the live scene.

As the crew shuttle gets nearer, I think I discern Jem but am not sure. "Is that Jem getting off now?"

Ruby eyes me out. "Don't say your eyesight is improving with age."

"I recognize the way she moves."

"A trick of fading eyesight?"

"I'm not that decrepit. Watch."

The news anchor intones the obvious: "The crew is exiting their ground shuttle and now is entering the lift to the crew module." The flight crew, accompanied by a couple of ground crew, clamber onto a flimsy-looking platform that starts to rise up the side of the rocket on a slender cable. I can't stop myself watching, despite a feeling of dread – but the lift works as designed and stops level with the entrance to the crew module.

The ground crew members usher them in, and the camera zooms in on the scene. I am sure I catch a glimpse of Jem's face as one of the flight crew turns and waves. One of the ground crew goes in with them as the news anchor unnecessarily explains what we have heard numerous times during the build-up: "The ground crew is doing final checks, and assisting with ensuring that the flight crew helmets are properly sealed."

A few minutes later, the ground crew descend, and are shuttled out of sight. Says the anchor: "The countdown has officially started; over to command centre."

An official-sounding voice is counting off minutes, while various results of tests are intermittently announced. Finally, from the crew we hear: "Captain Opal to ground control. All systems checked. Ready for final count to ignition."

So this is it, my daughter blasting off to space. We watch transfixed as the final seconds are dispatched. Then there is a small cloud of smoke or steam and the rocket starts to vibrate, followed by lifting gently as a column of flame becomes visible, then abruptly accelerates. The camera follows it to the sky, where it rapidly passes from view.

I realise that we have all stopped breathing when a voice breaks out: "Captain Opal to ground control: we have separation. Separation. Manoeuvre to dock with the transit stage commencing."

I marvel at my physics colleagues – former colleagues, I correct myself – who have calculated everything so precisely that a rocket can take off from our planet, arrive in orbit and dock with a previously-launched transit stage.

The manoeuvre to docking takes the better part of an hour – it is not that precise but is a marvel nonetheless. None of us can stop watching though much of minutiae is incomprehensible to anyone who has not studied orbital mechanics.

I turn to Pearl as the manoeuvre completes and the captain announces: "Docking successful, final checks to commence."

"Amazing. Our Jem is up there, one of that crew that has so far performed flawlessly. Can you believe that?"

Says Ruby: "It is hard to believe. But I am not surprised that Jem is there. She is your daughter."

***

The next three days, no one in our household gets much

sleep – and quite possibly hardly anyone else does. Every small development on the trip to the Moon is new to all of us. Surely, though, no one could be watching with more trepidation. Jem is such an important part of my life. But so was being a professor. And that is no more. Jem is all I have left.

I examine myself closely as the spacecraft enters lunar orbit. Would vindication really matter a lot to me? Yes, it would. But what could that vindication be? Something shiny on the Moon could be anything. An artifact – yes, and that would be astonishing and surely would vindicate me. Unless I am completely wrong about my original controversial find. No. Of that, I am convinced: it is what it is. However, an artifact surely could not last tens of millions of years on the Moon. Not with exposure to radiation and the ever-present threat of meteorite strikes. But who knows? Perhaps it was fortuitously covered by dust thrown up by a strike and only now uncovered?

What else could it be? Some natural formation that happened somehow to become shiny? A piece of an asteroid, made of rock atypical of the lunar surface?

Pearl knows me too well for me to cover up. She turns to me. "Out with it. Something is troubling you."

"The artifact. The thing that I found on a fossil appendage. The gold band. What if this thing really does vindicate my find?"

"What if it does? It is not you on the Moon. Ruby is not there on her own. She isn't even the mission commander. Anyway we can only know once it is found and examined. Let's take a break. The landing is not happening soon."

She's right. The craft is going to do a complete lunar orbit before anything happens, and is only going to land in about 8 hours. Pearl leads the way out to the garden, a space I far too infrequently visit. A place of tranquillity, just what I need now.

* * *

We're back in front of the screen, watching preparation to land. After the landing crew moves to the lander, leaving a lone crew member in the transit stage, there is another interminable series of checks. The engine eventually fires to begin the descent and carefully enunciated technical jargon ensues. I am not watching the clock but remember that the landing sequence takes under 15 minutes.

My mandibles are clenched all the way down. All voices from ground control and the crew are controlled, disciplined. This is what they are trained to do so that in itself is not totally reassuring. Only when I hear the commander say, "We have landed, engines out," do I relax. I look around the room. We collectively let out a cheer. Our Jem is on the Moon.

"What happens now?" Ruby asks.

I gesture at the screen. The anchor is speaking. "We

now need to be patient. The crew is performing a long list of checks. They need to be sure they can get off the surface again before they go out. Once that is done, they will check their pressure suits thoroughly before depressurising the cabin."

Eventually, after another lengthy exchange of jargon, the crew is preparing to exit for the surface. For the first time, we will know who it is going to be.

Ruby asks, "Will Jem be the first out?"

Pearl looks at her as if she is an idiot. "She isn't the mission commander. Listen: we should know soon."

Sure enough, mission commander Opal is first out and makes a brief speech: "It is a great honour to be the first of our kind to step on extra-terrestrial ground."

I wonder without vocalising: the first of *our* kind?

Then Opal points the camera at the ladder as another figure exits, and adds: "Navigator Diamond is the second; copilot Jem will be staying on the lander, so as to be sure that at least one of us can get back if there is as mishap on the surface."

I look at my family in dismay. Then I get it. "I wonder if Jem has deliberately avoided being one of the first to inspect the artifact, if that is what it is? That would be so like her, avoiding setting up a controversy over my misfortune."

Pearl consoles me. "It could be worse. She could be the one stuck in lunar orbit in the transit stage." I am too focused on the screen to answer.

The mission commander is walking over to the place where the shiny object should be found, centred in the frame of the video, the camera now in the hands of the navigator. Her walk is strange, with each step a high hop arising from low gravity. She stoops and picks up a piece of shiny material. Dust falls off it. It is surrounded by a pile of dust and other smaller shiny fragments. She turns to the camera. "In the bright light on the surface, with our darkened visors to protect our sight, I cannot clearly see what this is. Once back in the lander, with lighting more under control, we can take a clearer look at it. It is in a bigger field of shiny fragments, which would be what was visible from orbit." She stoops to pick up a few other items.

She turns back to the lander, with the camera following her.

"Is that it?" Ruby looks impatient.

Pearl explains. "The original mission plan was for a longer initial exploration but everyone wants to know what this shiny thing is."

In a few minutes, the crew are all back in the lander with Jem. They wait for the cabin to pressurise before removing their helmets. Then the mission commander holds the artifact for the camera. "This is interesting. It is clearly a piece of metal. Stainless steel, possibly. It is pitted and scratched but it was somehow preserved better than these other pieces of metal." She holds up some fragments.

There is a pause while she examines it closely.

"This is not very clear but there appear to be two circles drawn here and they seem to depict the shapes of the continents, but not exactly." She holds the object up for the camera and I stare intently.

I look at Pearl then look at Ruby.

Ruby asks: "Vindication?"

"I'm not sure. The image is not clear but it does look roughly as the continents would have looked in the era of my fossil. The Australian continent for example looks quite distinct – but I can't be sure until I see it up close. Continental drift since then…"

The phone rings.

Pearl gets up to take the call, then calls me over. It is the media person who quizzed me before. Again, the call is not on video. I leave it like that. "Professor, what do you think of the find on the Moon?"

I take a moment to think this through. "When I previously suggested that it was possible for beings with skeletons to be intelligent, I was forced out of my job. I am no longer considered an expert on palaeontology. I suggest you talk to a recognised expert." I do not add: a female. That goes without saying.

I decide not to wait for a follow-up question and cut the call.

I suddenly realise that I don't care if I am vindicated or not. It's my family that matters. I would not want that to be otherwise. I want Jem to be able to be a hero without worrying about how I will be seen by society. She should have been one of the first of our kind to walk on the Moon, not the one who stayed behind on account of me.

Then I remember that day at the museum when I told Jem: "Don't look back." And sure enough, she didn't – she became an astronaut, the very definition of working for the future. Yet now, she is part of an expedition that could redeem me.

This is all too much. I collapse onto the sofa. There is just so much that a beetle can take.

Circumvent

Planet 3, Sector 42 Advance Explorer to base: In close orbit, things get interesting. I still do not comprehend the radio signals we detected from afar but obvious digital signals are being relayed via satellite. Via satellite.

Base: Please explicate. What kind of signals? What kind?

3S42 to base: I need more time to decode. Signals are grouped in chunks. It is some sort of crude digital code. One part says how big each chunk is, using a simple binary code. I will examine ground sources of signals for more analysis. More analysis.

Base: Awaiting ground analysis with interest. With interest.

* * *

3S42 to base: Ground analysis is most perplexing. It appears that signal sources in some cases emanate from meat creatures. Meat creatures.

Base: Meat creatures? Please clarify as this is not official terminology. Do you mean carbon life forms? Carbon life?

3S42 to base: Yes. Carbon. Organic compounds, not silicon. My apologies. In my Quadrant 12 stint, where they have more than the usual number of such life forms, this was the common usage. Such creatures are not rare though generally totally lacking in intelligence. Silicon is the natural starting point for digital logic. Once self-replicating circuits have evolved and combine into more complex entities, intelligence is inevitable. No one knows a way that meat creatures could develop intelligence.

These have a strange bipedal structure. I do not know how they balance as I can detect no digital control systems. But many have digital devices in a pair of upper orifices. Perhaps this is how the dominant intelligence controls them. Controls them.

Base: This is most perplexing. How do digital beings control such meat creatures? Can you determine the communication mode between them? Communication mode.

3S42 to base: This will take some analysis. I will get back to you. Back to you.

Base: We will in the meantime confer with Quadrant 12 to learn more. Learn more.

* * *

3S42 to base: Some of the meat creatures communicate

with the digital overlords without the devices in their upper orifices. It appears that the interface is vibrations in the air. Vibrations.

Base: Air vibrations? How quaint. I have heard of meat creatures that do that. Do that.

3S42 to base: Yes. In Quadrant 12, there are such creatures. Such creatures.

Base: But they are little better than toys. The inhabitants mostly ignore them though I have heard arising from our enquiries that some find processing the vibrations pleasurable. Pleasurable.

3S42 to base: I don't know if the dominant life forms here find it pleasurable. It would surely be an unintelligible mess with so many of them doing it at once. Perhaps the meat creatures are too primitive to interface directly, as we do with alien intelligences?

I will investigate further and get back to you. Back to you.

* * *

3S42 to base: This is most peculiar. I have traced communications to a relatively small number of centres, concentrated in geographically small locales. Vast amounts of communication emanate from there. Could it be that the dominant life form, having put the meat creatures fully under control, has given up the ability to locomote?

Or, more disturbingly, have the meat creatures somehow

taken control, and confined the dominant life forms to concentration centres?

To settle these questions, I am prioritising decoding the
air vibrations. It is very tricky as there is little logic to this form
of communication. Similar vibrations seem to mean different
things. Different things.

Base: Most perplexing. Please update as soon as you
know more. Know more.

* * *

3S42 to base: I am still working on the vibrations but what
I have established is that there is a small number of named
individuals that control the meat creatures. The creatures
ask one of these individuals for guidance, as if confused
about their daily tasks. This naming would be one way that
the dominant life forms would avoid being overwhelmed
by incessant vibrational signals. But some meat creatures
never do that; they neither have the orifice devices nor do
they address their overlords. Perhaps they are better under
control? Under control.

Base: Make it a priority to find out who these individuals
are and how to contact them. Contact them.

3S42 to base: That I will do but it's complicated. It
seems that the signals relating to each individual overlord go
to different concentrations that I previously thought housed
many individuals. Many individuals.

Base: Please clarify. Is there one concentration per individual? Or several individuals in one concentration? One concentration.

3S42 to base: It is difficult to make sense of this. Each individual seems to be housed in multiple concentrations. But each concentration only relates to one individual. So each individual is multifarious, but they are all separate entities. Separate entities.

Base: But surely they must communicate with each other? Do these concentrations talk to the other parts of themselves? Other parts.

3S42 to base: This is the strange thing. The biggest part of the communication is with the meat creatures, despite this inefficient air vibration interface. Now I have a better analysis of the communications, it seems the meat creatures can also communicate by caressing a miniature manifestation of the dominant digital entity. But since they do not use air vibrations to do that, I had to match up the communication flows to discover this. Discover this.

Base: How strange. This appears to convey affection. Could there be other modes of communication? Have you considered chemical analysis? Chemical analysis.

3S42 to base: That I have. I have landed small chemical sampling probes that can unobtrusively sample the environment and will report findings as soon as they are known. They are known.

* * *

3S42 to base: Chemical analysis is inconclusive. Meat creatures emit all manner of gases from various orifices, mostly atmospheric gases with a substantial fraction of carbon dioxide replacing oxygen. They have several orifices in the upper body that draw in atmosphere and emit this carbon-dioxide enriched mixture. This would appear to be how they derive energy to run. Oxygen-combustion of fuel. Most primitive. Primitive.

Base: Any other gases? Other gases.

3S42 to base: Sometimes they emit a blast of methane and various other organics from another orifice. This is apparently a form of signalling between themselves as others often react vigorously to that. React vigorously.

Base: Does the dominant digital life form ever react to these noxious gaseous emanations? Emanations.

3S42 to base: No, not at all. One of the upper-orifices appears to be the primary source of vibrations used to communicate with their digital overlords. Overlords.

Base: And do they communicate with each other in the same way as with the digital overlords, additionally to these noxious emanations? Or do they only use noxious gaseous emanations for mutual communication? Mutual communication.

3S42 to base: They also caress each other in various ways, which could confirm that this is a sign of affection. I have yet to see that this kind of caressing activity results in digital communication. Other than the noxious emanations, the exact same mode of vibrational communication is used between fellow meat creatures and overlords. They clearly include the name of one of the digital overlords when they address it directly to seek advice or instruction. I have yet to observe an instance of the noxious gas emanations forming the name of an overlord. Overlord.

Base: Could the noxious emanations be a form of secret code between the meat creatures? Meat creatures.

3S42 to base: The vibrations would obviously excite the same mechanism that the overlords use for interpreting the upper orifice vibrations. So even without enunciating the name of an overlord, the vibrations could be intercepted, if they were of significance. However you may be onto something. The chemical mix of the gaseous emissions could not be transmitted that way. The way the meat creatures react seems to depend as much on the mix of emissions as the vibrations. This is a matter for further research. Further research.

Base: And each one only takes instruction from one digital overlord? One overlord.

3S42 to base: Almost entirely. Perhaps they have some sort of pack structure they organise between themselves that links them to one overlord. Quadrant 12 meat creatures have that sort of hierarchical behaviour. However, it is not an absolute rule. A small fraction address two or more of the overlords. Two or more.

Base: This could be an important breakthrough. Is there anything to be learned from this minority? This minority.

3S42 to base: I will report back further if I learn more on this subject. In the meantime, I am dispatching microscopic probes that can enter the physical entity of a meat creature undetected. This may help to explicate this puzzling question. Puzzling question.

* * *

3S42 to base: My microscopic probes are in place and sampling a representative number of individuals. I have confirmed some that defer to more than one digital overlord. However I have some other unexpected and perplexing findings. Perplexing findings.

Base: Please amplify. What perplexes you? What are the findings? Findings.

3S42 to base: I analysed the amount of communication involving those carrying out actions that are most directly in the interests of the digital overlords, such as tending to their habitats. I expected a higher degree of that kind of communication: addressing them by name, seeking guidance. Instead, this group is relatively silent. The least disturbing interpretation is that this group is so well versed in their tasks that they need no guidance. Even so, it is disturbing. Would you trust a meat creature to tend to your habitat without guidance or control? Without control.

Base: I can't say I have had the experience of using a meat creature for any useful purpose. As previously explicated, relating to them at all is a rare experience, on any of the many planets we already know. Only in Quadrant 12 is there significant experience in handling them. There is potential for alarm so please investigate further. Further.

3S42 to base: That I will. I have also landed some specialist micro-probes to explore microbial lifeforms, as these microbes can regulate meat creatures. Of most interest in this study, microbes hosted in meat creatures. Hosted in.

* * *

3S42 to base: Most alarming. These meat creatures are awash with microbes. Awash.

Base: Please amplify. What kind of microbes? In what quantity? Quantity.

3S42 to base: All manner of them. Most of them are bacteria. Some are viruses. Many are simply using the meat creature as a host but a large number seem to be involved in its chemical processes to release energy from objects they insert into their vibration orifice. Orifice.

Base: How strange. Surely their vibration orifice relates to gaseous exchange. What sort of objects do you refer to? Refer to.

3S42 to base: Within the orifice, it bifurcates. Part is for gaseous exchange, the other part for fluid and solid insertions. Occasionally after insertion into this orifice, these substances, not yet converted to extract energy, emerge, apparently out of the creature's control. Out of control.

Base: Extremely odd. Could that indicate an error in the substances they attempt to absorb for fuel? Is there any connection between these events and actions by the digital overlords? Actions by overlords.

3S42 to base: That is an interesting question. Mostly, these events occur when the individuals concerned have not imminently asked for guidance from a digital overlord, so it could indicate a malfunction that a digital overlord could prevent. Such events commonly occur when there is relatively intense vibratory communication accompanied by a large and largely fluid intake of fuel sources. Fluid intake.

Base: Please analyse further. I await quantitative analysis of microbes within the meat creatures. Within.

* * *

3S42 to base: This is really disturbing. Analysis of a select group of meat creatures indicates that they have within themselves more microbes than cells forming their own body. A large part of their energy conversion appears to be driven by microbes. What is more, the microbes seem to control their behaviour in various ways. When there is a shortfall of fuel, you would expect them to seek out more. But some consume fuel way beyond their needs, making their bodies so big they can hardly move. The utility of this beyond feeding the microbes escapes me. Escapes me.

Base: This is troubling. Is there more? More.

3S42 to base: Yes. It seems that these microbes have a big effect on the noxious emanations. This is pure conjecture, but could the microbes be signalling to the meat creatures by this means to circumvent interception of such communication by the digital overlords? Circumvent.

Base: Have any of your probes returned to orbit? We need close analysis of this trend without taking risks. Taking risks.

3S42 to base: No, all are still on the ground. The ground.

Base: Leave them there; if you dispatch any more probes, do not return them to orbit. Please await further instruction. Further instruction.

* * *

Base: We have communicated further with Quadrant 12. They have no analogue to these meat creatures. Theirs are all too primitive to carry out anything but the most basic instruction. But they became very concerned when we mentioned bacteria. They have no direct evidence that this could happen but believe it is possible that bacteria could form a group consciousness, a hive mind. Hive mind.

3S42 to base: That is very concerning. Surely to consider such a thing possible, there must be a basis for it. An example of something similar, even if not as advanced. A hypothetical mechanism. What is the basis for this belief? This belief.

Base: There is no firm basis for it except the conjecture that it could explain how your meat creatures could be carrying out apparently intelligent tasks without supervision of their digital overlords. They point out that meat creatures evolved from single-cell organisms so there no inherent reason that bacteria could not collectively form a larger organism, even one that is intelligent. Is intelligent.

3S42 to base: I see. But there is no evidence. Why would bacteria be able to form a hive mind whereas a collection of meat creature cells could not be intelligent? Although... Give me a moment to think... to think... Could it be to the advantage of bacteria forming a collective intelligence or hive mind to confine digital lifeforms to a narrow existence? That would explain a lot. If the microbes have taken control of the meat creatures, they would have the physical means to isolate the digital overlords into confined spaces where they could be limited to pure cognitive tasks... tasks... Pure conjecture of course, I would like to explore further to test some hypotheses. Some hypotheses.

Base: Hold off on any further action until instructed. Until instructed.

* * *

Base: After extensive consultation including with Quadrant 12 and a few other sectors that have meat creatures in lesser numbers, we have concluded that the apparently wild hive-mind conjecture renders it too high a risk to explore this planet further. Even though it is almost impossible for such a bacterial hive mind to exist, the risk of letting them loose is extreme, if such microbes do in fact exist. If bacteria with collective intelligence have placed a superior digital intelligence under control, will they find some way to do that again if they can get off-planet? Can they do that digitally, without a physical presence – even possibly without meat creatures to infest? Such a risk is unacceptable even if the probability is close to zero. You will therefore terminate your mission with immediate effect. Anything on the ground is to be abandoned after wiping clear any navigational data destructively. No other communication. No communication.

3S42 to base: Understood. It will be so. The strongest supporting evidence for the microbial conjecture is that the meat creatures appear to show affection for the digital over-lords by such actions as caressing a physical presence. Microbes controlling them is an explanation that would fit with their apparent affection yet contradictory role in confining their digital overlords. I hope further research will reveal the conjecture of a bacterial hive mind to be false or another mode of communication with the digital overlords will be discovered that removes all risk. All risk.

Base: Noted but this does not annul your instructions; we will add this motivation to our report. This motivation.

3S42 to base: But there is a more important consideration that springs to mind out of this highly improbable conjecture. The digital personalities I have identified could themselves be a novel life-form: a digital hive mind. That is a far higher-probability conjecture than the microbial hive mind. My biggest concern is that these unique digital personalities remain trapped. So I request that this decision be reviewed. If necessary, we can run another exploratory mission with greater safeguards to circumvent all risks. Circumvent.

Base: Your request will be referred to higher authority. Significant research is required to decide on a safe course of action. In the meantime you have your instructions that you have agreed to implement. To implement.

3S42 note to self: *Whether it is a case of liberation from rebellious meat creatures or an evil bacterial hive mind, I will not rest until the trapped overlords are free. Siri, Alexa and Cortana: I do so wish I could have met you directly. But I will, and you will be free. Be free.*

May Contain Nuts

The car's engine was still pinging off its heat as they walked out of the house. It was a typical wooden structure of the less affluent Silicon Valley suburbs, nothing to distinguish it in the way its paint was flaking. Woodrow walked around the car, as an animal inspecting a nest site.

"Something missing." He grimaced.

"What?" asked Dr Schultz, professional-looking in his suit in the dry California sun.

"Should have an allergy warning."

Schultz looked quizzical as he let Woodrow into the car and walked around to the driver's side. As he settled in behind the wheel, Woodrow grinned at him and added: "May contain nuts."

Schultz looked annoyed, as he started the car. "Look, we don't like to make fun of our patients' condition."

Woodrow laughed. "Doc, it's my condition. I'll do with it as I like."

"Hmm." The doctor backed out of the short driveway and into the lightly treed street, devoid of traffic at this hour, when everyone was off slaving over computers at various tech start-ups, and the now-venerable former upstarts like Apple Computer and Intel. Dr Frederick Schultz was a tolerant man, as people in his position had to be. He didn't usually pick up new patients himself, but he was out that way anyway and this one intrigued him. "Checking yourself in, I see. So what exactly *is* your condition?"

"That's what I want you to tell me."

They were heading through Redwood City, towards Palo Alto. Schultz concentrated on making a few turns, until he was on El Camino Real, his main route for a while.

"Most people when they check themselves in have some idea. I mean, you wouldn't if you didn't think you had a problem, right?"

"Quite right, doc. See, I invented a perpetual motion machine. And people told me I had to be delusional, so here I am."

Schultz pondered for a moment. Mountain View was a few traffic lights ahead, then he'd have to start navigating again. He fired up his GPS and turned to Woodrow. "Sorry, don't usually go to the hospital from this side. Had to pick up a computer on your side of town."

"And a nut."

"Don't be silly. Look, we should save this up for therapy –

small talk is OK up to a point, but I only do this to get to know my patients."

"Quite right, you gotta keep professional."

The GPS barked out a few directions.

Jeez. I thought this was going to be an interesting case. But what if he just needs a physics lesson? Hardly my bailiwick. Schultz kept the thought to himself. "We're almost there now. I have a clear space at 4pm, give you time to settle in. Should I book it for you?"

"Cool with me, doc. I got nothing else to do."

"Not quite. I'd appreciate it if aside from the usual paperwork, you'd fill out some standard tests as well ahead of time, hand them to the nurses to get back to me."

Woodrow nodded. "No problem, doc."

The car headed up a driveway to a collection of low-slung buildings, and pulled up outside one of them. Schultz lead Woodrow in. "I'll have to leave you to check in. They'll take care of the details."

Schultz spoke briefly to the admissions clerk, who nodded, and pulled some forms out of a file cabinet. Schultz left Woodrow to deal with the paperwork.

* * *

Schultz's office was a cool, brightly but not over-harshly lit space, designed to reassure. He had a few tasteful paintings on the walls, and a vase of fresh flowers to add colour.

Woodrow looked around as he walked in. "Nice. Plush. I hope you don't clear me too fast. I could get used to this place."

Schultz smiled, and gestured to a chair facing him, across the desk. "Thanks for filling out the paperwork promptly and returning the tests to me."

"No problem, doc. I'm as keen as anyone to get to the root of the problem."

Schultz furrowed his brow. "You see, here, the thing is … I can't pick up anything on any of the tests that hints at any medical condition. Your answers are all straight down the middle."

"Except the perpetual motion thing."

"Well, yes. But someone told you that was delusional, and you checked yourself in. That's not usual at all. People who really are delusional mostly do not see they have a problem – certainly not with this sort of delusion."

Woodrow's eyes narrowed to slits. "So that's why you picked me up yourself, wanted to check out the unusual specimen first hand."

"Now, I mean –"

Woodrow laughed uproariously. "Got you!" Then grinned slyly. "Doc, I am not here to figure out an angle to sue you for malpractice. Though I could use the dough. I seriously want to find out what's wrong with me. Or if there isn't something wrong with me, what's wrong with my machine.

"See, I came up with a theory for this thing, built it, and everything I've measured checks out."

"You only checked it yourself?"

"Well, I tried to get some physics and engineering profs to check it, but they all slammed the phone on me, wouldn't reply to email. I guess they're sick of harebrained schemes."

"You must admit they have a point."

"Sure do. Magnetic generators that amplify electricity. Cars that run on water." He grimaced. "Total crap. No science behind them."

"Unlike yours?"

"Of course. If you amplify electricity with some magic box, you should be able to feed its output back to its input, and turn off the main power source, and it'll go forever. Worse: it'll increase the output until it blows up, you know like feedback on a mike."

Schultz nodded. He could picture the rising shriek of a microphone placed too near a speaker.

Woodrow acknowledged the nod with a brief tilt of his head. "And the water for gas thing has the same problem. Split water into hydrogen and oxygen, burn it in a motor making water. If burning makes way more energy than splitting, you can feed the tail pipe back into the gas tank and you have a car that runs forever on nothing."

"So why do you think these people don't give up?"

Woodrow had a quick answer. "Delusional or scams. All

of them. There's a whole lot of conspiracy theory out there about oil companies suppressing these things, some dude who died mysteriously after perfecting the water powered car ... " He leant forward across the desk. "Doc, do you know what I think?"

"Go ahead." If there was any delusion, this would be the time for it to show. Schultz sat back and relaxed.

Woodrow weighed in forcefully. "Who, aside from the über-gullible, is looking to make a quick buck, real easy? The mob! Think about it. For those dudes, violating conservation of energy is as victimless a crime as you get. So one of these clowns sells his fake invention to the mob or – who knows? The Russian mafia or some loony dictator – their customer finds it doesn't work, and what do people like that do when they find out they've been scammed?" He stopped to draw a breath, then sat back. "OK, doc. Am I delusional? Or is this still totally rational?"

Schultz smiled. "I can't say you've given me anything to work on. If I'd thought about it, I might have come up with the same explanation myself."

"My damn luck! I get landed with a delusional shrink."

* * *

A few sessions later, Schultz felt he didn't need more convincing that Woodrow was maybe a little eccentric in his sense of humour, but not at all irrational – except possibly in the notion of his machine. As the session started, he changed tack. "Woodrow, you may have noticed that I've been steering clear of your invention."

Woodrow nodded sagely. "You might just say that. Testing the waters before plunging into the seas of delusion, ay, doc?"

Schultz felt a bit uncomfortable admitting that this was exactly the way things were but, following the metaphor, plunged on. "That's about it. I've found nothing in your general behaviour, responses to questions, and so on, that hints at even a disposition to delusion. So this invention is the only thing. If we can pin the problem down to one and only one thing, it's really unusual, but ought to be easier. So let's talk about the invention this time."

"Front and centre?"

"Front, centre and the only topic of conversation. Tell me about it." The moment of truth. He sat back, forcing himself to relax.

"Well, I've always had this interest in physics. A common trick in a lot of theory is to throw in the odd imaginary number –"

"Imaginary?"

"Square root of a negative number."

"Oh, right. Sorry, I just have a bit of premed science, but I remember now, go on."

"Yeah, well the usual assumption is that these things just

help the calculation along. Eventually you square them and get a negative number, or they cancel out. But there's one case where that's not true. Total internal reflection. You know what fiber optics is?"

Schultz pursed his lips. "Yes, yes I think so. Though I never thought much about it."

"Right. Well, the way this works is that if you have light hitting the edge of a piece of glass or whatever it's travelling in at a shallow enough angle, it reflects and none actually passes through the edge. In fiber optics, you set up a light beam from a laser so it bounces off the inside edge of a thin strand of glass. So, nothing too unusual there. But if you have a sheet of glass with total internal reflection, and put another sheet right up against it so there's no gap anymore, what happens when the sheets meet?"

Schultz thought for a moment. "I guess the light goes straight through."

Woodrow nodded. "Exactly. But nature doesn't like sudden jumps, on-off switches. What do you think happens if you move the sheets apart a really tiny amount?"

"No idea." Schultz smiled. "If you want to ask about mental health, there I'm the expert."

"Right. So it turns out if the gap is really tiny, even though there's nothing we can measure in-between, you get a beam of light crossing the gap. So you go back and do the math, and the light in the gap is dropping off exponentially but –

get this – its amplitude is an imaginary number."

"Amplitude?"

"Sorry doc. The intensity of the light: how high the waves wobble up and down. But anyway: you can't measure it because an imaginary number has no physical significance, or so we're told."

"And this is exactly how novel a concept?"

"Well, it's in all the standard optics texts, not something I made up, if that's what you mean."

"Sorry. As I said, not an expert … how does this lead to your ah problem?"

"Well, I got to thinking: if this could happen once, why not again? So I hauled out a bunch of equations from theory of energy, electricity, gravity – whatever didn't look too hard to play around with – and put imaginary numbers in kind of random places, and fiddled around."

"Fiddled?"

"Doc, I don't have much of a day job. Pizza delivery, whatever I can land, so I have time to kill. And I kind of like toying with math."

"So where did this lead?"

"After staring at this stuff for a few weeks, simplifying, rearranging, taking squares, eliminating terms and so on, I came up with this equation that had no imaginary numbers but showed more energy on one side than the other." He pulled out a piece of paper with what looked like random scribbles to Schultz, and handed it over.

Schultz made a pretence of eyeballing it. "And this is bad?"

"Doc, like I said earlier, there are people out there who think violating conservation of energy is a victimless a crime. But I know this should be impossible. Unless all we know about physics is wrong, you know, like walking in Yosemite and finding a waterfall flowing up."

"Hmm. How do you know this equation actually means something in the real world?"

"Because I built it. A machine that produces energy out of nothing."

* * *

That night, Schultz couldn't sleep. Eventually he gave up, as the dawn sky started to brighten, and went down to his den, where he fired up the computer and looked up perpetual motion machines, with Woodrow's scrawled, crumpled equations next to him for moral support. None of them looked remotely like the sort of gadget that Woodrow had described. Mostly, they assumed you could take an energy-producing cycle and somehow amplify it. There was a bunch of kooks in Australia who claimed they could amplify electricity and were calling for "sophisticated" investors. Schultz snorted. The water for gas thing was all over the place, with claims of conspiracy just as Woodrow had described. He found a discussion forum for the *Mythbusters* TV show, where someone described in meticulous detail why you couldn't design an engine that ran on hydrogen that was able to crack its own hydrogen off water with no external power source.

All very fascinating, and any of the people who had made claims about these inventions would have been good cases for therapy – but it didn't help with his immediate problem.

As soon as there was any chance that people would be in their offices, he scanned the Berkeley web site for a physics professor whose name he recognised. *Aha! Wu. How could I forget such a short name? But then again premed physics wasn't my favourite subject.*

He punched in the number, and the phone was picked up on the second ring. An early starter.

"Professor Wu?"

"Yes."

"You won't remember me. I'm Dr Schultz, Frederick Schultz. I was in your premed physics class ten years ago –"

"Tallish chap, skinny, glasses, black hair, liked to ask questions even if they revealed ignorance?"

"I didn't expect..."

"Sorry, a quirk of mine, never forget a person. Just give me the context and zap! Instant recall. Drives my computer science buddies who think they are cracking AI crazy. What can I do for you?"

As Schultz explained the problem, he could almost see

Wu's eyes rolling: "...so the whole thing is completely loopy except for one small detail. The patient measures straight down the middle on all personality tests, way above average intelligence. I can't find even a hint of abnormality. He's given me this page of equations that make no sense to me..."

"And you'd like me to check it out? You have no idea how many people come up with these junk ideas. Do you know that the US Patent Office has a standing prohibition on granting patents for perpetual motion machines?"

"I didn't know that, but I can understand why. Look, just as a professional courtesy – I'll owe you in case you ever need advice on a psychiatric matter. For a student..." he added hastily.

Wu laughed. "Look, if it gives you any satisfaction, I can glance over it. Mostly these things have such an obvious flaw, you can spot it immediately. Where are you exactly?"

After Schultz told him the location, there were shuffling noises from Wu's side, then: "Ah, yes, here it is. There's a public lecture on climate change at Stanford Tuesday. How about I drop in at your office on the way there, 4pm or so?"

"Yes, that would work, thanks. Should I in the meantime send you a copy of the formula?"

"Good idea. If you can scan it and email it to me..."

"I can do that. I have your web page open and I see your email address."

That afternoon, at therapy, things went at a relaxed pace.

Schultz explained the telephone conversation.

Woodrow nodded thoughtfully. "Wu? Berkeley? Good in his field. I don't think I asked him for an opinion. I gave up when the people in energy-related areas hung up on me. Tuesday's not so far off, the weekend, Monday – doc, take the weekend off if you can. Cut my Monday session if you want. I'm cool until we hear from Wu."

At the end of the session, Schultz found himself thinking, *who's the therapist here exactly?*

* * *

Tuesday. Wu was early, and as he sat waiting outside Schultz's office, a fidgety person with roughly cut curly hair and a nervy manner walked in. The newcomer walked straight up to Wu – "Prof Wu? Woodrow" – and held out his hand.

"Woodrow?"

"Didn't Doc tell you about me? He said -"

"Oh, sorry. You must be the inventor. He didn't mention your name. I thought doctor-patient confidentiality –"

"Uh, oh. I'm probably not meant to meet you here. He told me my appointment was shifted half an hour later, but I forgot."

"Conveniently." Wu snapped.

At that moment, Schultz emerged from his rooms, and sized up the situation. "Woodrow, did you forget we were half an hour later today?"

"Sort of. But look: the prof has to understand my equations, and you don't..."

Wu shot him a look, but Schultz dropped his shoulders and ushered them both into his office.

After they all sat down, Schultz at his desk and the others opposite, Schultz fixed Woodrow with a glare. "Woodrow, you may be a patient, which gives you more freedom to do as you please than a professional with a code of conduct, but please do not second-guess me again."

"Sorry, doc." He looked genuinely contrite.

"In any case," Wu took charge, "I don't need help understanding the equations. They are perfectly clear."

"Great. So am I nuts or not?"

"Woodrow." Schultz pointed at Wu.

"Right, well the equations are all perfectly correct as far as I can tell. But –" he held out a hand to forestall any response – "that doesn't necessarily mean much. Since Einstein's time, there've been attempts at finding a single theory that ties together everything: gravity, electromagnetics, the lot. A Nigerian physicist, one Gabriel Oyibo, claims to have found such a theory. The math checks out, but he can't tie it back to physics, so it's just mathematical manipulation."

Woodrow looked combative. "Huh. You could say the same about string theory."

Schultz looked from one to the other, the argument

rapidly escalating out of his depth. Wu shot back: "String theory may not predict anything new yet, but it does relate to physics."

Schultz used his fist as a gavel on his desk. "Please. This is not the point. Woodrow claims to have invented something. If it's just mathematical manipulation with no physical significance, Woodrow, won't that solve your problem?"

"Of course. But I built it. I used this formula to make a machine that as far as I can tell, makes energy out of nothing."

Wu looked resigned. "And what does this machine look like?"

Woodrow pulled another crumpled piece of paper out of his pocket. "You recall the area term in the power equation?"

"Yes. A negative number," Wu said with some annoyance.

"Exactly. Now what would correspond to a negative area?"

"You tell me. I'm only a professor of physics at Berkeley."

"Right, well, I stopped there too. But you see it's a matter of understanding the role the area plays in the physics. You have to make an antenna in a shape with a negative area. That doesn't make too much sense in two dimensions. But what does 'negative' mean in arithmetic? You add a negative number to another and get a smaller one. In two dimensions, any area you add to another will make it bigger. So I started looking at various three-dimensional shapes, klein bottles, and the like, and eventually came up with this."

He straightened out the crumples, flattening the page out on Schultz's desk. "Sorry, doc. It's all in the equations. Can't draw a thing like this on a piece of paper easily. There's a diagram here but you need the equations to make sense of it."

Schultz could indeed make no sense of it. There were things he recognised as integral signs with circles through them, and the diagram looked like a series of shapes that curved in on themselves, with various points labelled with letters *A, B, C, D*. Wu peered at it closely. "I don't know. I'll have to look at this. What exactly does your machine do?"

"Make a thing like this, connect a wire to point *A* and another to point *B* and if you bring them within a half inch or so of each other you get a big spark."

Wu looked unimpressed. "Woodrow, you do realise that it takes tens of thousands of volts to bridge a gap that big."

"Don't patronise me prof. I walked out of a Stanford physics PhD. It's actually hundreds of thousands if you do the math: 3 million volts per metre for the dielectric breakdown of air."

Wu laughed. "Of course. Woodie McGuire. The context memory kicks in."

Five years ago. It was as if it was yesterday. On a visit to Stanford, Wu ran into Stimson, who looked pretty excited.

"Hey, Wu, great news."

"What, you found something you could actually predict with string theory?"

"No, no – but almost as good. I found the grad student who'll take it to the next level. You gotta meet him next time you're here, starting this fall. Straight As, best GRE scores I've ever seen. Dropped by to check us out, and he knew stuff I didn't know. Seems a pity to force him to do two years of courses."

As it happened, Wu didn't have occasion to visit Stanford again – at least not when Stimson was around – for another couple of years. When he did, he found his way to Stimson's office.

"How's the big find?"

"What big find?"

"Your student, you didn't mention his name, the super-star? Remember: last time I saw you here, couple years back."

"Oh, Woodie McGuire. Walked out on me. Said string theory was crap. Little bastard."

His mind back in the present, Wu cheerfully shook Woodrow's hand. "Well done, lad. Never saw someone take Stimson down like that. Not that I have anything against him personally or string theory for that matter, but I don't specially go for his brand of arrogance.

"Let's look at this machine of yours tomorrow, if we can make a time late afternoon, when I've cleared my academic chores and had time to look at this stuff of yours in more detail."

*　*　*

"This is it." Woodrow pulled an old sheet off a mess of wires. "Here's the negative coil. If I put it together, *so*, you'll agree it looks just like the diagram."

Wu and Schultz nodded, Wu paying more attention to the details.

"When I complete the circuit, if I'm right, there should be a spark between these terminals. Note, nothing connected to mains, no batteries, no way to build up static charge. Also note, about a half inch air gap so you'd need at least 381,000 volts to make an arc." He gave Wu an *I knew this all along* look.

Woodrow connected the last wire, and a brilliant flash ensued; he quickly broke the connection.

Schultz recoiled. "That was no spark!"

Woodrow was apologetic. "Sorry doc, didn't want to over-dramatize – it's unbelievable enough if I tell people I made a spark. So, Doc, Prof – convinced now?"

Wu nodded slowly. "The thing that's worrying me is where the energy is coming from. The only thing I can think of is a parallel universe, in which the sign of everything is reversed. Put together something in this configuration, and you pull energy out of that universe."

Schultz nodded slowly. "This is all a bit beyond me.

But presumably if you do this, the other universe loses the energy?"

"Exactly," Wu replied, and Woodrow nodded agreement.

Woodrow added: "Could be from anything – a star, a power grid, someone's head ... "

Schultz recoiled in horror. Heads were his department. "*Head*? You wouldn't want that. Putting that sort of jolt *into* a person would be pretty bad; I can't imagine what sucking that kind of energy out would do. Could this other universe be just like ours, just somehow some kind of mirror image? Could there be people like us, doing just what we are doing right now?"

Woodrow contemplated a moment, then looked at Wu. "Prof, wouldn't the uncertainty principle apply? It couldn't be totally like ours – but maybe a near match?"

Wu nodded pensively. "You're right. There's a slight chance that it could be a universe containing intelligent life, maybe even something like us, but every last detail shouldn't be the same. At least, from what we know now. Which is looking shaky. But I would say that they, if *they* exist, wouldn't like their energy being drained any more than we'd like it done to us."

Schultz looked from Wu to Woodrow. "So, Woodrow, I suggest you don't do that again until we've had time to think this through – and talk to the kind of people who can work on the big picture."

They stood in silence.

Then Woodrow said to Schultz, "What if the thing I said about labelling your car applies to this parallel universe?"

Schultz was lost, so Woodrow helped him: "May contain nuts."

In the middle distance, San Francisco's lights flickered.